TANGLED HEARTS

The Harts of Texas: Book Two

BARBARA MCMAHON

One

Brianna Hart looked up as he filled the doorway and her heart caught, her breath stopped. For an endless spiral down time, everything stood still.

He hadn't changed.

Yes, he had. He appeared harder, older, tougher. He'd always been tall. Now, in the heavy winter coat, he seemed gigantic. He topped six feet by several inches. His broad shoulders still looked as if they could carry the weight of the world. Yet his size had never intimidated her. He'd always been heart-stoppingly gorgeous, with his sinfully dark hair and piercing black eyes.

In that, at least, he hadn't changed. Neither had the stubborn jut of his jaw, or the intense manner he used to focus his full attention on someone to the exclusion of everything else.

He focused that attention on her.

His eyes were cold, harsh, and seemed to peer right into her soul. Gone was the softness she'd glimpsed once or twice long ago. Gone was the amusement that had often danced in his dark eyes. Now he regarded her as a stranger.

"Are you the one who called about the break-in?" he asked, his eyes flicking quickly to Martha Benson, her neighbor, back just as quickly to her, holding her gaze as if he'd never released it.

Brianna nodded, afraid to trust her voice. She hadn't expected Jake Morgan to respond to the police call. He was a detective, not a beat cop. Not anymore. Did he like his new job? Though she guessed it wasn't that new by now. He'd just gotten the promotion when—

"Here?" He glanced around the tidy living room, his eyes missing nothing. Coming back, they studied Brianna.

She shook her head and slowly rose. Tearing her gaze from his, she smiled politely to Martha.

"Thanks for letting me wait here. I'll let you know what they find out," she told her neighbor.

"Okay, Brianna. Come back if you don't want to stay home alone tonight." Martha said. She and her husband, Sam, had insisted she wait with them until the police arrived.

Brianna had found the front door to her small house broken open. A quick glimpse had been enough for her to see her living room had been trashed. Fleeing to the safety of her neighbor's without entering her own place, she'd called the authorities.

Since no immediate danger seemed evident, the dispatcher had said she'd send someone as soon as an officer freed up. There'd been an accident on the highway and most of the officers on duty were responding to that.

Clearing her throat nervously, Brianna smiled at

Martha as she passed to lead Jake to her place. Agonizingly aware of every inch of the man, she was extremely careful to refrain from even brushing lightly against him. It wasn't easy. She longed to feast her gaze on him, drink in the very sight of him. It had been more than two years since she'd last seen him. Two long, endless, lonely years.

But who's counting.

She kept her gaze forward and focused on the doorway leading to the cold winter night. An unexpected cold snap had blanketed the area of east Texas. A few inches of snow had even fallen.

She tilted her chin in a parody of confidence, hoping she could fake it enough to fool him. A woman had to cling to some pride when a man dumped her. Especially when she never knew why.

"I live two doors down," she said as they reached the cleared sidewalk. Snow had been piled high on the curb when the snowplows had done their jobs. The small mound bordering the walkway on the lawn side looked insignificant in comparison. Most of the row houses were dark. Part of a large complex on the outskirts of Texarkana, all were fairly new. Brianna had been thrilled when she found she could afford one of the smaller units. It was a safe neighborhood. She never expected a break-in. And not in her house. She had nothing to tempt a burglar.

Their footsteps crunched on the icy sidewalk, their breaths hung suspended before them in vapor clouds of pale white. Despite the freezing temperature, Brianna's blood heated from proximity to the man walking so closely beside her.

"When did you discover it?' Jake asked, falling into step beside her, careful to keep a certain distance between them. His steps were measured and deliberate. He moved smoothly like a tiger on the prowl. He always had. She remembered feeling protected by it once. Now it seemed faintly threatening.

"I arrived home about seven tonight. I spent Christmas with Jase and his new wife, Shannon. When I reached my front door, I could see it had been forced open, the lock broken. The door was slightly ajar, not much. It didn't register at first. What it meant, I mean. I pushed the door and turned on the lights before I saw the mess. Then I went to Martha's to call the police."

"Smart. Never go into a house that's been burgled until you know it's safe."

He'd told her that before, when he'd cared about her, worried about her living alone. He'd told her many things to keep her safe. Only he hadn't been able to tell her anything to keep her heart safe from the devastation and pain he'd caused when he stopped calling.

"I remember," she said softly.

"Damn." His voice was so low she wasn't sure he really spoke.

"Are you back on patrol?" Brianna asked as she hesitated before the open door of her town house. She hated to go inside and see the damage that had been done. She'd been so proud of her home. From what she'd glimpsed earlier, it was now utter chaos. Stalling wouldn't change anything but maybe it would help her cope a bit better. And she needed help if she had to deal with seeing Jake again, as well.

"No. I was on my way home when the call came in. I heard about the accident on the highway so I swung by just to check—on the off chance the guy might still be here. The regular patrol should be here in a minute or two." Jake pushed past her to examine the destruction in the living room.

He stood still and let his eyes roam around the room. She knew he recognized some of the furniture from the apartment she'd lived in when he'd known her. Other things were obviously new. He studied them for a long moment. Everything was tumbled or tipped over, but the rampant destruction so common with vandals was not evident.

"How long were you gone?" he asked, walking farther into the room, throwing a quick glance at her, then looking away. He didn't want to look at her. He didn't want to see how pretty she looked in her burgundy sweater, her long, slender legs encased in black wool pants. Didn't want to notice how her honey blond hair gleamed in the bright overhead light, longer now than when he'd known her.

He especially didn't want to look into her sky blue eyes. He'd been lost once before in those eyes. Never again!

He didn't want to be within a mile of her, if the truth be known. He clenched his teeth. The sooner the patrol showed, the better. This was strictly business. What had passed between them was best left in the past.

"I was gone six days," she said, her eyes wide as she stared blankly at the mess.

"So this could have happened at any time over the past week."

He moved on to the kitchen. It hadn't been touched. The short hall to the left led to a bedroom and bath. The bedroom had been tossed, as well. He paused in the doorway, trying to assess the damage without touching anything. The large bed was new. He quickly moved his gaze. The room was full of feminine clutter that seemed so foreign in his very male world.

"My guess is it wasn't vandals but someone looking for money," Jake said as he reentered the living room. Brianna hadn't moved. She stood near the door, her expression bleak as she surveyed the scattered books, the jagged screen of her computer and the overturned tables and chairs.

"Looks like vandals to me. They smashed my computer."

"After we dust for prints, you can check the place out to see if anything is missing—"

"Hey, Morgan, slumming? I didn't hear there was a need for the big boys here. Thought this was just a routine B and E." A tall man in uniform stood in the doorway, smiling.

Brianna turned suddenly at the new voice. Relaxing slightly, she watched as the patrol cop entered and introduced himself as Don Winston.

"I was on my way home and heard the call. Thought maybe the perp might be nearby, but this could have happened as long as a week ago." Jake moved easily toward the door, his manner undergoing an immediate change.

Brianna watched intrigued as he relaxed, the friendship with his co-worker evident. It was a sharp contrast to the cool remoteness with which he treated her.

"What happened?" Don asked, looking around.

"I don't have much. Brianna Hart is the victim. Came home from a trip and found it like this." Jake shrugged, his gaze surveying the room once more, pausing only briefly on Brianna's face.

"I'll take over now, thanks. We'll see you at the New Year's Eve shindig, won't we? You bringing Diane?" Officer Winston drew a leather-covered notebook from his pocket.

Brianna's gaze swung sharply to Jake.

He nodded as he headed for the door. "Yeah. Save us a seat if you and Heather get there first. See you." Without another word or another glance at Brianna, he left.

Brianna watched him leave, her heart beating heavily in her chest. Her breathing was still erratic. She tried to blame it on the disruption to her life by the break-in.

Diane.

She closed her eyes briefly, wondering if the pain would always be with her. *He was seeing someone else.*

Should she have been surprised? He was the most decidedly male individual she'd ever known. And she'd known plenty. Raised on a ranch not too far from Texarkana, she'd been surrounded by macho cowboys and wranglers from birth. Her two older brothers were both strong, virile men. But in her eyes Jake had them beat six ways to Sunday.

He'd probably been dating all along, ever since he'd last called her. But it hurt. She'd loved the man, adored him, thought he walked on water. She'd even started to believe he cared for her.

Then presto, one day he didn't call. And never had since. No explanation, no easing down. Nothing.

"Sorry you have to go over everything again, Miss Hart, but if you could fill me in on what happened, we'll see what we can do." The police officer held a pen poised over a small notebook.

The night seemed endless. The questions were easy, but she knew very little. Once the fingerprinting had been taken care of, she was permitted to set her things to rights. While doing so, she tried to determine what, if anything, was missing.

But her concentration faltered. She could not focus on the task. It centered squarely on Jake Morgan. As she had endless times before, she wondered what had happened to end their relationship. She'd been crazy about the man and had thought, in his own way, he'd been crazy about her.

Granted, he'd never been as demonstrative as she. In his line of work, trust and frivolity came rarely. He'd seen things she'd never even dreamed about. But there'd been a spark between them, a growing closeness that she'd cherished.

Where had it gone wrong?

"Nothing appears to be missing from here," Brianna said as she put the last pillow in place on her bed.

The police officer dogged her footsteps through every inch of her place, asked her again to verify nothing had been taken.

"Nothing?" He sounded baffled.

"I can't find my backup disks and external drive, but nothing else is missing. Not that I can see. And the only things really damaged were my computer and the two books where the spines were broken." It could have been so much worse.

"Hello?" A male voice called from the front door.

Brianna followed the policeman to the living room, peering around him. For a second, she thought Jake had returned. Instead, a locksmith stood in the open door.

"I got a call that you needed emergency repairs tonight," he said genially, his hand already running down the damaged door near the broken lock.

"Yes, I do, as you can see. Who called?" Brianna rubbed her forehead. She would have to get the lock fixed before she'd feel safe again. Thank goodness the man was already here.

"Some cop called." The man shrugged, examining the splintered wood where the lock had given way. "I can fix this right up for you. Won't take more than half an hour." With that he set to work.

"That's it for me, then, Miss Hart," Officer Winston told her some time later. "I'll call you if I find out anything or have any more questions. If you discover anything else missing, let me know."

"Thank you." Brianna sank down on the sofa while she waited for the locksmith to repair her door. The policeman had checked all the other doors and windows for her; nothing else had been tampered with.

She felt violated. Her home, her sanctuary had been

invaded. It would be a long time before she would feel comfortable here, knowing some stranger had been through her things. Knowing the lock on the door could so easily be broken. She'd never had to worry about such a thing on the ranch. The door was left unlocked so no need to break in. But with cowboys and cattle dogs and all the activity, a burglar would have a hard time breaching that house.

When the door had been repaired and the locksmith left, Brianna continued to ramble around her place. She hated to turn out the lights—which was stupid. The house was secured, and whoever had trashed her place was long gone with no reason to return. All the damage had been done.

The phone rang, sounding unnaturally loud in the stillness of the night.

"Hello," she said, snatching it up. Anything to postpone going to bed.

"You all right?" The familiar voice seeped through her like fine whiskey, deep and dark and a bit rough. How many other nights had he called late, when he'd gotten off a shift and wanted to talk? She closed her eyes and let the bittersweet memories flow through her.

She swallowed, old longings rising fast and hot.

"Yes. Thank you for checking," she said politely.

"The locksmith finish?"

"Are you the one who called him?" A warmth flooded through her at his thoughtfulness, even as tears pricked behind her lids.

"No big deal. You have a lot on your mind with this, I'm sure. It's not your normal welcome home."

"No. Thank you. I wouldn't have thought about it until I was ready to lock up. This way, the police officer was still here when he arrived so I had someone with me the whole time until the door was secure again."

"Anything missing?"

"No." She couldn't let it end there. In only seconds he'd hang up. And it would probably be at least another two years before she saw him again or talked to him. Or maybe there'd never be a next time.

"I didn't expect to see you tonight," she said, longing to keep the lines of communication open if only for a few moments longer. She wanted to lap up his deep voice, to relish the shimmers of excitement from hearing it. If nothing else, it chased away some of the fear.

"I didn't know you moved. Last I knew, you still lived over on Sheridan Avenue."

"I moved about eighteen months ago."

Had he known, would he have ignored the call? Let the other cop be the first on the scene? She was afraid to ask him, afraid of his answer. "Are you still at the same place?"

"Yeah. Listen, I'm glad your door got fixed. Chances are the guy broke in the first night you were away and has been long gone since then. You'll be fine." His tone became more impersonal, more distant.

"Yes." He was reassuring them both she'd be safe, then he'd pull away like before. And she still didn't know why.

"Call 9-1-1 if you hear anything or get scared."

"Yes. I—" There was nothing else to say. "Goodbye, Jake. Thanks for calling."

Brianna woke the next morning after a restless night's sleep. It wasn't only the break-in that had kept her awake; it was seeing Jake again. She dressed warmly in dark wool slacks and a bright blue sweater, then brushed her long hair until it crackled with static electricity. Toast was all she wanted for breakfast. And coffee. She didn't feel much like eating.

As she sipped her second cup, she wandered back to her living room and stood almost where she had last night. She could picture Jake there, prowling around, looking for clues to assist in apprehending the person who had broken into her place. Curiously, she wondered what he'd thought of her home. Had he connected it to her at all in any personal way? Or was it just another crime scene to him?

And who was Diane? How serious were they? Would he stop seeing Diane as suddenly as he had stopped seeing her, or was he more involved this time?

Shaking her head impatiently, Brianna finished her coffee and briskly began to make plans to contact her insurance company, replace her computer and clean her house from top to bottom to get rid of all the fingerprint powder. She'd put Jake Morgan behind her two years ago. Seeing him briefly last night wasn't going to miraculously change anything.

The house shone when Brianna finished and she was pleasantly tired. Surely tonight she'd sleep.

Tomorrow she'd have to begin her lesson plans. After destroying her computer hard drive, the vandals had then absconded with her backup disks and external drive. As the newest assistant professor of mathematics at the community college in town, she prided herself on being prepared. She had mapped out her courses during the past summer and had thought herself on top of things. Now she was back to square one. Or square two anyway. Some of her preliminary notes were in her office at the college. Tomorrow she'd go pick them up. At least she had a starting point.

She had told the police what was on her computer. Would they start looking at students? Who else would care about lesson plans and grades for college classes?

The knock on the door was unexpected. Nervous, she used the peephole for the first time. Recognition was instant.

"Jake?" She opened the door, startled to see him again. After two years of silence, twice in two days?

"Hi, Brie. Can I come in?"

"Sure." She stepped back, her eyes fastened on him. There was no way she could stop the spontaneous curl of heat that seeing him ignited, but she could control her reactions around him. Pasting a polite smile on her face, she took a deep breath and held it, trying desperately to look as remote and detached as he did.

"Everything's back to normal, I see," he said, standing near the sofa. He dominated the room, his very presence seeming to fill it with excitement and masculine power.

Brianna nodded, afraid to step too close lest she be

scorched by his heat.

"Anything missing?"

She shrugged. "They broke the computer and stole my backup disks and external drive. Other than that, nothing. And it's such a pain. I had all my lesson plans on the computer. I have to start over and classes begin again next week."

"Tough break. But it could have been worse. Does Don suspect it was kids looking for exams or grades or something?"

She shook her head, wishing she could step away. His eyes were dark, seeking. She hoped he didn't see more than she wanted him to see. "I don't keep exams grades here. I've already turned in the grades from last semester. I don't keep anything important from work here, just lesson plans. The college's computer security is high, so of course I use that."

He shrugged, his eyes never leaving hers. "Students don't necessarily know that."

"Maybe at the beginning of each school year I should announce that to all my classes," she said lightly, suddenly wishing she could bring a hint of amusement to those assessing eyes, a hint of softness to the hard glare that never deviated an inch.

Instead, he merely nodded. "Might be a good idea."

She shook her head and relaxed as much as her racing heart would allow. "Do you want come coffee?"

He hesitated a long moment, as if weighing the pros and cons before finally nodding slightly.

"I'll get it. You could take off your coat if you're staying awhile." She hurried to the kitchen, feeling as fluttery as a freshman dating a senior. What was the matter with her? He was an old friend.

Friend?

Well, more than that, but if she didn't want to set herself up for future heartache, she'd better remember he hadn't wanted it that way and had ended it. Nothing had changed since the last time she'd seen him.

So why was he here?

Jake shrugged out of his heavy coat and tossed it across the back of her sofa. Prowling around the room, he loosened his tie as a further concession to comfort. He'd had a twelve-hour shift and was tired. But he wanted to make sure she was all right before he headed for home.

He paused by her desk and studied the wrecked laptop. Whoever had damaged it had wanted to make sure it would never work again. The screen had been bashed in. The base looked as if it had been hacked, the keys ripped off. Was there a particular reason, or was it just wanton vandalism? Had the guy been interrupted after damaging the computer? Why wasn't there more damage throughout the house?

Slowly he turned, his glance taking in the rest of the room. It was warm and welcoming. As Brie had been the entire time they dated, warm and welcoming—always happy to see him.

Moving on, he stopped by her bookshelves, smiling at all the mystery titles.

She'd always been a mystery buff. Once, a long time ago, he'd wondered if that was why she'd liked dating a cop. He hadn't thought about that in a long time.

He spotted a group of photos. Her brother, Josh, he recognized instantly, his expression tightening as his gaze moved to the next photo. The man looked a bit like Brianna in a rugged way. He must be her brother, Jase. Was the petite woman with him his new wife? The faded picture to one side had to be her parents, the couple who had died when she'd been a little girl.

"So why did you come, Jake?" Brianna asked as she stepped into the room and deposited the tray of coffee carefully on the table in front of the sofa.

"I wanted to make sure you were all right," he said, turning and crossing the room to sit on the chair near the table.

"You could have checked with Officer Winston. Isn't he the one in charge? He could have told you I'm fine." She handed him a cup, sweetened and black. She remembered how he liked it.

"There's fine and there's fine. I wanted to make sure," he repeated, watching her over the rim of the cup as he took a sip. It was hot, but not as hot as she made him feel. Coming here had been a mistake.

"Actually, I'm more angry than anything right now. I'm incensed that someone had the nerve to break into my home. Furious that they touched my things, destroyed my work. And irate that I don't have a clue as to who did it so I could hold them accountable," she said, flaring up.

"Better anger than depression or fear," he said. She was pretty when she was mad, her eyes like blue flames, her cheeks rosy and flushed.

"Fear? Oh, about staying here, you mean?"

He nodded.

"I guess." She sighed heavily, calming slightly. "I'm not going to let some crook run me out of my home. There's nothing to do but go on."

As she had when he stopped calling.

She'd tried to call him a couple of times. But when she'd been given the runaround at his office, she'd known not to call again. Gripping her hands tightly around her mug, she sipped her coffee.

She ached to know what he had been doing these past two years, longed to know if he had missed her at all. But she refused to ask a single question lest she never be able to stop.

Jake stood abruptly. "Thanks for the coffee. I'm glad you're doing okay after all." He grabbed his coat when she stood.

"Thanks for stopping by." She tilted her chin again, as she had the night before. She refused to break down and beg him to stay. He had made his decision two years ago. Why, she still didn't know, but it didn't matter. He was no longer hers. He never had been.

Despite her best attempts, however, when she opened the door, her hand brushed against him involuntarily. Her fingers skimmed his sleeve, feeling the rock-hard muscles bunch tightly. She closed her eyes briefly at the shock of sensation that flooded through her.

"Take care, Brie," he said huskily as he passed by and out into the cold night. No kiss, no hug, no words of future meetings. Simply *take care*. Yet it was more than she had received last time.

Drifting off to sleep later, Brianna was vaguely pleased to acknowledge she'd not given any indication to Jake of how much his leaving had devastated her. She ignored the loneliness in the big bed that she had once thought to share with a hot, passionate male. She was over him. Or she would be one day soon. Very soon! She had lesson plans to worry about now, not some tall, rugged cop.

Brianna bought a new laptop first thing the next morning. She had another week before classes began and she needed to work flat out to make sure she was ready for the first day. Her job as associate professor in the mathematics department had been hard won. She worked hard to make sure she performed so well that there would never be any question that the decision had been the best the college had made. She had her eye on a full professorship before she reached thirty.

After purchasing the computer, Brianna headed for the campus. Fall classes had ended before the Christmas break, but there were always students wandering the campus, some working on a thesis or long-term projects, taking advantage of the Christmas break to take advantage of the enrichment part of campus. Others were just hanging around for any action they could find.

Brianna smiled as she made her way to her office. Only a few years ago, she'd been an undergraduate at a different college. How she'd loved it. So much that Jase had once accused her of wanting to become a professional student. That wasn't her goal. She liked the synergy of college students. She'd made the switch from student to instructor then assistant professor with little difficulty. And she still loved the discussions and arguments that could arise as young brains forged forward with new ideas and fascinating conjectures.

The office building echoed eerily when she entered. The usual professors, instructors and endless groups of students were missing because of the holidays. Even the administrative staff was gone until next week. Her footsteps echoed in the oddly silent building.

She hurried up the stairs to the small cubicle she called her home away from home. It had a narrow window that gave a brief glimpse of the campus. Scarcely large enough for her desk, bookshelves, large chalkboard and a couple of chairs, it still represented the first step up the ladder toward a full professorship. And she was lucky enough to have it all to herself.

Brianna opened the door and stopped dead.

Two

"I'm trying to reach Detective Jake Morgan," Brianna said yet again. This was the third voice to come on the phone. How hard was it to get through if someone had an emergency?

Or was he deliberately avoiding her? Was he worried she'd call him on the slightest pretext to try to insinuate herself back into his life—

"Yeah, this is Morgan." His distinctive Western drawl was more welcome than she anticipated.

"Jake, it's Brianna. I'm sorry to bother you at work and all, even though it is police business. Well, it's really probably more for Officer Winston, but I don't think his area extends over here and the campus police did say they'd handle it and contact the city police, so I—"

"Brianna!"

"Yes?" She took a deep breath, holding on to her nerves with a will of iron.

"Take a deep breath and slowly tell me why you're calling. Slowly." The order came through loud and clear.

Brianna took another deep breath. "I did. I thought I did. Jake, my office was ransacked like my house."

"I'll be there in ten minutes," he said, severing the

connection.

Slowly, Brianna placed the receiver carefully back on her phone. She tried a shaky smile for the elderly security guard standing beside her desk. "He's coming over," she said.

"Campus police won't like it, miss. They said they'd handle it," the man said morosely.

"Yes, well, Detective Morgan is a personal friend."

And she was beginning to feel she needed one. It was cold in her office. The window had been cracked open. Scattered files and folders, torn papers and ripped books added to the chill. She stood and headed for the door.

"I'll wait outside for my friend," she said, not waiting for agreement, giving in to a need to escape.

She sat on the marble bench in front of the building, willing the rays of the bright winter sun to warm her. Cool, crisp air swirled slowly around, cold enough to keep the snow from melting, to keep the sun from offering any solace beyond an illusion of warmth. Still, she felt better sitting outside than in her office.

Who would do such a thing? The security guard had checked the other offices on the floor. None had been disturbed. It was only hers. She knew the drill from last night. Wait for the police to check it out, then ascertain if anything was missing. Then clean up everything.

Instead of working on lesson plans for the first few days, she'd spend the day putting things away and salvaging what she could.

She hoped she could find her notes for the spring classes and that her grading sheets and student files weren't impossibly scrambled. But for the moment she just wanted to sit in the sun and forget the scenes of destruction that had met her ever since her return from Christmas vacation.

Jake careened around the corner in front of the student union. He drew to a halt before the Ross Building, against the flow of traffic, his light flashing. Climbing from the car, he left the lights on, immediately headed for her, as out of place on the college campus as a fox in a hen house. His tall frame moved easily through the scattered groups of undergraduates with a controlled motion that reminded Brianna of a wolf on the prowl. King of the wolf pack, dominant, arrogant, confident and deadly, he made the strutting college boys look like pups.

Yet he remained totally oblivious to it, his eyes already on her. All his attention focused on her.

Willing her heart rate to slow, Brianna sprang up from the bench and waited impatiently for him to reach her. She couldn't take her eyes away from his dark gleam. For one heartbeat she felt safe. Jake would find out what was going on and make things come right. She knew it.

Then the shivers of awareness began, raking through her as he drew nearer and nearer until she could reach out and touch him. She didn't have to.

He reached for her first, drawing her up firmly against his hard chest, holding her in his arms while she breathed out a shaky sigh of relief, resting her forehead against his shoulder.

"Oh, Jake. I know it isn't your case and I probably should have called Officer Winston, but I wanted you. I didn't know what else to do."

"You're shaking." His arms tightened even more until she could feel the steel in him along the length of her, feel the imprint of masculine strength surround her.

"It's the last time I take a trip, I can tell you," she said, trying for some humor. Truth to tell, she felt just the tiniest bit scared.

"Where's your office?" He released her, held her shoulders while he ducked his head to stare down into her blue eyes. "Do the campus police have any ideas when it happened?" he asked, ever the cop.

"They don't know. Some time since school let out before Christmas. It's this way."

She felt momentarily bereft when his hands dropped from her shoulders, but one arm came around her and while she longed to leaned against him to savor his strength, she pulled away. Drawing on her own determination and courage, she led the way inside and to her office.

The elderly security man stood on duty, leaning against the hallway wall. Except for the door to Brianna's office, all the others on the floor were closed.

"This is Detective Morgan. He wants to see my office," Brianna said as they drew abreast of the open door.

"Now, miss, there's no need. The campus police have been and gone. They have the case in hand," the older man protested.

Jake smiled easily, offering his hand to the guard. "I'm not planning to run interference, just checking it out for Miss Hart. I won't touch a thing."

"I'm sure that won't matter. The place has been dusted, pictures taken. She can clean it up now if she wants. I'm just waiting around until she's ready to leave. The lock on the door's busted so I don't want her to be alone."

"Nice of you. I can take over if you have other things to do," Jake offered.

After a sharp look at Jake and a quick glance at Brianna, the older man nodded. "You'd probably do her a whole lot more good than me if there was a problem." He nodded and saluted Brianna with two fingers before heading down the hall.

Jake swung back to her, the smile gone, his expression pure business. "Let's see."

She stood aside as he prowled her office. Since the campus police had already dusted for fingerprints, he had no hesitation in picking things up and examining them.

"Anything missing?"

She shrugged. "Not at first glance. But it will take days to get this mess cleaned up and put back into order. Much longer than it took at home if they've scrambled the papers."

"Any other office hit?"

"No. The campus police checked when they were here."

He leaned back against her desk and stared around the small room for a long moment, then snapped his gaze toward her.

"All right, let's have it, Brie. What do you have that someone wants?"

"Nothing!"

"A break-in at home and one at your office in the same week. That stretches coincidence a bit too far. You must have something someone wants pretty badly."

"I don't." She glanced at the mess again before peering thoughtfully at her computer. Unlike the one at home, this one had not been damaged. "But someone might think I do, I guess," she said slowly.

"Like what?"

She hesitated. She knew she could trust Jake with her life, if necessary. But she wasn't sure how much she should tell anyone until she'd spoken with her boss.

"Actually, I need to talk to someone else."

"What the hell do you mean you need to talk to someone else? You called me the minute you ran into trouble. Now you want to talk to someone else? Who?"

"I can't say." She swallowed hard.

Tension grew as he stared down at her. She could feel the sparks. She should have anticipated this and, as a precaution, should have called to get clearance. At the very least, she should have notified them what had happened.

Only she'd never considered that anyone would think she had classified materials with her.

"Isn't it a little late to be thinking about the boyfriend?" Jake snarled.

"Boyfriend?" She blinked. Was that a joke? She hadn't had a date in over two years, and he thought she had a boyfriend?

Why would he care if she did? He'd made it abundantly clear he no longer wanted to be considered in that role. What about Diane?

He reached across and grabbed her arms, drawing her up close. His dark eyes were hard and narrowed as he leaned over until his nose almost touched hers. "I'm the one you called first, sweetheart. I'm the one who can help you, not some boyfriend you only just remember now."

She blinked, feeling the soft kiss of his breath fan across her cheeks. Her gaze took in the deep depths of his eyes accented with the faint lines that radiated from the corners, the high bones of his cheeks, the tight control he held on his mouth.

She licked her lips, wishing he'd kiss her once more as he had long ago. If she reached up a scant four inches, she could brush her lips against his, taste him again, absorb the searing heat he generated against her skin for another second of eternity.

"It's classified," she squeaked, drawing on all her reserves to keep from moving that short distance.

Shimmering waves of desire swept through her. Blood heated through her veins and the roar in her ears almost deafened her. For years her brothers had tried to give her everything she wanted, but she'd never wanted anything as much as a single kiss from this one man.

Time hung suspended as the world narrowed to only Brianna and Jake, blue eyes staring deep into black ones. Their hearts pounded in sync, their breaths mingling, uniting as one.

He moved first, straightening and setting her back. Waiting only long enough to make sure she hadn't lost her balance before releasing her, he stepped away, arching one eyebrow.

"Classified?"

She nodded. "About a year and a half ago, I was hired by the Strategic Air Command to do contract work in cryptography at Barksdale Air Force Base," she said, referring to the air base in nearby Louisiana.

"You crack codes?"

She smiled at that. "More along the lines of encrypting than deciphering. It, uh, goes hand in hand with math."

"And you think someone might be looking for these codes in your possession?"

"Which is really stupid. I wouldn't take anything from the site, much less leave it carelessly around my house or office."

"Maybe whoever is behind this doesn't necessarily know that."

"Then they can't be too smart. I think it's more likely to be your student theory. I should check in and let my boss know what's happened."

"How often do you work there?"

"It's on an as-needed basis. I finished my last assignment just before Thanksgiving. They haven't called me for the next one yet."

"How did you find out about working for them?" he asked, leaning back against the wall and crossing his arms as he stared across her office out the window.

"How? There was an invitation to alums of UT, an ad sort of. I applied and they ran a background check and then hired me."

"When?" His gaze pierced her, his concentration

formidable.

"Eighteen months ago." Suddenly she felt as if she were being interrogated. Why? She had done nothing wrong.

"Isn't that when you said you got your new place?"

"It was the extra money that enabled me to afford it."

She pulled her cell from her pocket and tapped on her boss's number. Turning slightly for an illusion of privacy, Brianna went through the officer on duty and reached Colonel Shaefer. She quickly explained what had happened and offered Jake's theory of a disgruntled student as a possible explanation.

"Well?" Jake asked when she hung up.

"He said to keep him apprised. For the time being, he's willing to let it stay in civilian hands. Especially since he knows nothing's been taken from the base."

"What happened eighteen months ago that caused you to change your life, get a new home, take on additional work? Love affair gone bad?" Jake asked softly.

She glanced up, then shook her head in defense. There was no way she would give him the satisfaction of knowing how much he'd hurt her when he left. No way would she give him a clue.

"Just time to change things. I need to get some order out of this mess. I probably shouldn't have called you. I think the security guard was correct. The campus police—"

His fingers covered her lips, stopping the flow of words. Brianna shivered, stepping back to break contact.

"I'll see you home. The building is practically deserted and I'm not leaving you here alone. Get what you need and we'll go. You can come back when the staff returns."

"I remember how bossy you could be," she mumbled, kneeling down to stack papers together, piling them in such a way she could carry them home. She'd spend the evening sorting and trying to restore order. And there were still the lessons to plan.

"Bossy? This coming from the prima donna herself, who expected every man she knew to jump through hoops pleasing her?"

"That's not true." She flashed him a sassy grin. "If the man in question wanted to jump, who was I to stop him?"

Jake's smile hit her like a lightning bolt. Slow and sexy, it spun her senses until she was reeling. She reacted as if he'd touched her. She found herself smiling back at him as she felt the strong pull of physical attraction between them. He practically oozed masculine appeal. He was too potent to just spring on someone. She needed time and space to work up a resistance strong enough to withstand that blatant virility.

"Yeah, well, maybe your breathing makes men want to jump."

"Right." Dragging her gaze away, she stacked more papers. *That's why you left two years ago.*

"What are you planning to do with all those?" he asked, stooping down to her level.

"Take them home to sort. I can't start work next week with this mess. I need to get it all in some kind of order before school starts again."

"Wait until the staff gets back."

"No, I can get a lot done over the next few days."

"Tomorrow's New Year's Eve."

"So?" she said. Remembering Diane and the date she'd heard confirmed, Brianna wished he hadn't mentioned it.

"So what are you doing? A hot date?"

She shook her head, keeping her gaze firmly on the pages she was sorting. Her face grew stiff trying to hold a neutral expression. She should *not* have called him.

His fingers reached for her chin and tilted her head to face him. "No hot date?"

"No date, hot or otherwise," she said in a whisper.

If he said one disparaging thing, she'd dump the stack of papers on him and storm out. It was no longer any of his business what she did with her nights.

His thumb gently caressed her lower lip, brushing back and forth slowly as his eyes tracked its journey. "Brie honey, he isn't worth it."

She could scarcely think. His touch drove her crazy—crazy with longings, yearnings that evolved from deep within and clamored to be assuaged.

"Who?" she whispered, mesmerized by the soft touch of his thumb, the heat from his body, the scent filling her nostrils. She wanted nothing more than to spend the rest of her life with this man.

"The bastard who hurt you. Don't hide away from things because of him."

She blinked and sat back on her heels, pulling away from his hand. He watched her warily. He hadn't a clue that he was the man who had hurt her! She couldn't believe it. He sat there and advised her against himself. She almost wanted to laugh. If she hadn't wanted to cry so much she might have.

Scrambling to her feet, she picked up the papers she'd already gathered. "You don't need to worry about me, Jake. I'm managing just fine. I like my life the way it is," she lied. She dumped the stack on her desk, then frantically gathered up another pile.

"Brianna--"

"Really, Jake. I'm fine. Go on and have fun tomorrow with Diane." She closed her eyes in anguish. She hadn't said that, had she? Someone please tell her she hadn't said that. Oh, lord, couldn't the floor swallow her up?

"How do you know about Diane?" His voice was cool.

"I heard it somewhere. I'm ready. If you'll just give me a hand to my car, I can manage from there. I'm sure I'll be all right at home. I have the new lock and the bad guys won't be coming back. There's nothing there they would be interested in and—"

His finger stopped the words again.

"I'll see you home."

Brianna remained silent as they walked down the deserted halls, conscious of her footsteps echoing loudly while she could scarcely hear Jake's silent tread. She thanked him politely as he delivered the stacks of papers to the passenger side, then held her car door open. She slammed it shut and started the engine right away. She wanted to get home, close her door and be alone.

He stayed right behind her during the short drive home. He was out of his car and over to hers before she could gather up all her papers. He accompanied her up the walkway, never touching, yet seeming to surround her completely. In other circumstances, she'd have welcomed his attentiveness. Now she wanted him to leave.

"Thanks for seeing me home," she said, refusing to look at him lest her feelings showed.

"Call me if anything else happens," he ordered.

She shrugged. "What else could?"

"Call me!"

She took a deep breath, nodded for the sake of expediency in getting rid of him, her eyes firmly on the knot of his tie.

But when he captured her face in the warm palms of his hands, she was lost. He raised her up for his kiss, his lips warm and firm, moving in a long-remembered caress that excited and soothed, that inflamed and enticed. Brianna responded instantly, like gasoline to a match. Heat flared and consumed her. She wanted more, wanted to step into his embrace, encircle his neck with her arms and press herself against him in a mating as old as time. She ached with wanting him to open her mouth with his and plunge into the welcome she'd so gladly offer. She yearned for him to touch her with hot hands that would learn her secrets and teach her new ones. She wished he wanted her as desperately as she wanted him.

But he pulled back after a brief kiss, his eyes flickering, his expression giving nothing away.

"Happy New Year, Brie," he said.

She watched as he walked away, her heart pounding, her cheeks flushed and hot. She wished she had nerve enough to call him back. Yet she knew he wouldn't come. He'd left two years ago after all. Nothing had changed. Slowly she entered her house.

Brianna spent the next two days sorting papers. She found notes for classes, grading sheets for students, drafts for journal articles all mixed together in the piles she'd collected. Sorting everything kept her occupied, kept her from thinking about Jake.

New Year's Eve she went to bed just after ten. Trying desperately not to imagine Jake and his date at some party, trying to pretend she didn't mind being home alone on another New Year's Eve, she climbed into bed with a mystery she'd been wanting to read. It couldn't hold her attention. Finally she dozed off, murder mixing with dancing and Jake pursuing the killer and then her.

The phone rang. Blinking, Brianna awakened and reached for it. She frowned. It was after midnight. She'd fallen asleep with the lights on.

"Hello?"

"Happy New Year, Brie." The deep, familiar voice warmed her to her toes.

"Happy New Year, Jake," she said softly, closing her eyes to better savor the happiness that bubbled up at his call. "Where are you?"

"I'm at the policeman's ball. Where are you?"

"In bed."

"Alone?" he asked sharply.

She giggled a little, then caught her bottom lip with

her teeth to keep from crying. "Yes, not that it's any business of yours. And you're with Diane."

"I'd asked her a while ago. She's just a friend, Brie."

She started, suddenly wide-awake. Jake was not one to give explanations. Why explain this? She would much rather have had an explanation two years ago. How did he expect her to respond?

"Is it a nice party?"

"As these things go. They start off fine, then the guys get down to talking shop."

"Is Diane with the police department?"

"You don't want to know about Diane, Brie. Were you asleep?"

"I was reading."

"A mystery?"

"Of course, what else?"

In the background, Brianna could hear someone call Jake. The woman's voice sounded full of laughter.

"I've got to go."

"Happy New Year, Jake. Thanks for calling."

Brianna hung up in total confusion.

Why had he called? If he hadn't happened to respond to her call about the break-in, she wouldn't have seen him again. He hadn't said anything about seeing her socially.

Yet it seemed a very personal thing, calling to wish her a happy New Year so soon after midnight. Especially when he was on a date with another woman.

She knew she'd never understand him in a thousand years. Giving up, she snuggled down and soon fell back to sleep.

Two days later, the classes resumed. Brianna went to work early, anxious to get her office cleaned up now that the rest of the staff was back to work. The building resounded with the calls of students, the click of high heels, the stomp of boots.

The bustle was common and comforting. She plunged into the mess, determined to get it all under control as quickly as she could.

Brianna glanced at the clock from time to time. She wiped her hands on her wool slacks and stared out her small window. It had been repaired. The sun shone in. It made the room feel warmer.

She planned to invite Jake to dinner, to thank him for coming to her rescue, so to speak. As soon as she gathered enough courage to call him.

The idea had come to her when she awoke New Year's Day. She'd wanted to call right away, then decided she'd better think the invitation through first. She didn't want to make it seem more than it was, merely a thank-you for his help.

Right. If that was all she wanted, she could send him a card. How long had she been staring out the window? She darted another look at the clock. He'd be at work by now if he wasn't already out in the field somewhere. No time like the present to call.

In a minute.

Finally, chiding herself for her foolishness and cowardice, she tapped in the number. Taking a deep breath, she pinned a bright smile on her face, hoping it would help her sound carefree and casual when she issued the invitation.

"Morgan," he growled.

"Jake, it's Brianna."

There was a moment's silence on the other end. "Another break-in?" he asked.

"No. Everything's fine. Actually, I was calling to invite you to dinner Friday night." She said it in a rush. She grimaced. She'd meant to be calm and casual. Too late now. She held her breath, awaiting his answer.

The silence ticked by slowly. Brianna could hear her heart beat, slow, nervous, heavy. The bright smile faded. He was going to refuse.

"I don't think so, Brie, but thanks," he said at last.

"Okay. It was just a thought. I meant it as a thank-you for coming over when my office was broken into. No big deal." Her throat ached with disappointment.

"It's part of the service, ma'am." He was all cop.

"Right. Nice to know Texarkana's finest are so prompt when called for help. Thanks again." She tapped end before she made even a bigger fool of herself.

She looked up at the ceiling, blinking furiously. She would not cry over the rejection. Going into the call, she'd known he probably wouldn't want to see her again, unless she needed a policeman, of course.

Slowly she rubbed the ache in her chest. She was used to it now. She'd had it in one form or another for two years. But sometimes it still hurt fiercely. And after his attention the past few days, she might have been excused for thinking he might come for a simple thank-you dinner.

The phone on her desk rang. She jumped at the unexpected sound and looked at it resentfully. Gathering up her notebook and purse, she let it ring as she headed out to her first class. She'd be early, but the walk would calm her down and she could get started putting some of the problems on the blackboard before the students drifted in. She had work to do. She couldn't be fretting over a tall, dark man who had already left her once before.

Where was she? She'd just called. Wasn't she at work? Jake slammed down the receiver.

It was just as well. He had no business seeing her for dinner. It would remind him too much of other dinners they had shared, of other evenings spent together. Yet he'd heard the disappointment in her voice.

He wouldn't have deliberately hurt her for the world.

Three

Brianna recognized his car as soon as she turned onto her street. What was Jake doing here? He'd made his feelings very clear on the phone earlier. Now what?

Something about the investigation?

Reluctantly she pulled into her driveway and stopped. What she really wanted to do was turn around and drive until she ran out of gas, but that was hardly a mature way to handle this. Taking a deep breath, she wondered if maturity was overrated.

He'd left his car while she dithered and was at the door of hers before she knew it. Opening it, she shivered slightly in the cold air. The late-afternoon sun was but a memory; dusk was falling fast and with it the temperature. It would be another cold night.

"Brianna."

"Hi, Jake. What an unexpected surprise. Was there something more on the investigation you needed? I thought Officer Winston was the one handling things. I assumed you filled him in on the situation at my office last week." She couldn't get the words out fast enough.

"Brie, shut up. You talk a lot when you're nervous, did you know that?"

She glared at him. Of course she knew it. But she didn't like that he'd also recognized the fact. "Why would I be nervous?"

"You tell me."

"If I was the tiniest bit nervous, it could only be because of all the problems recently. I mean, how often does a person have her house broken into and then her office. I was lucky to have my car with me or it probably would have—"

He leaned over and kissed her.

Her lips clung to his, all protestations forgotten. The cold faded and a delicious warmth pervaded. Slowly, as if in a trance, Brianna dropped her books and briefcase and purse. She slipped her hands up around his neck, pulling him closer.

His arms encircled her and drew her snug against his long length. His mouth moved against hers until she opened to him, reveling in the taste so long denied. When his tongue skimmed her lower lip, she moaned softly in supplication. She wanted more. She was spinning out of control and didn't care a whit. Her tongue danced with his.

When he eased back a bit, Brianna realized her coat was open, as was his. They had pushed them apart to press closer. She had no desire to move an inch unless it was to close the gap he'd created.

"Don't be nervous around me." Jake's voice was low and seductive. His breath brushed across her damp lips, warming them in the rapidly cooling night air.

"Jake, I'm not nervous. I was merely saying—"

Again he cut her off with a kiss, deepening this one

until Brianna forgot where she was, forgot what she should be doing. The only reality was Jake in a spinning universe that spiraled in wondrous delight. She strained to get closer, to offer him the same heady delights he provided. Her mouth moved against his, her tongue mating in a rhythm as old as time. Her hands threaded themselves through his thick pelt of hair, relishing the texture, testing the length.

His heat scorched her, made her coat superfluous. Gone was the numbing cold of the winter; gone was the hard concrete beneath her feet. She floated on a warm, tropical cloud of blissful sensation. Shimmering waves of electricity sparked along her nerve endings, bringing remembered pleasure so long forfeit.

"It was always hot between us," Jake mumbled, lifting his hands up to cup her face, dropping little kisses against her lips, across her cheeks, tilting her face to trail kisses along her jaw, down her throat.

"It was always wonderful," she replied, eyes closed to better savor every stroke of his touch. She could go on forever. Could he?

"I didn't come for this," he said, swooping back to capture her lips for another kiss. Was he lying to himself?

He straightened and reluctantly dropped his hands.

Brianna blinked, crashing back to reality in a rush. Embarrassed at her ready compliance, she bent to retrieve her books and purse. Searching for her keys, she turned to head for the door, conscious of Jake only inches away. She couldn't look at him. Did he mean to imply she'd thrown herself at him?

"Just why did you come?" she asked as she walked to the door, her head held high. She would not apologize. He'd kissed her after all. She'd only gone along for the ride—for the dizzy, spiraling, heart-stopping ride. She still felt his warmth.

Once inside, she shrugged out of her coat and hung it in the closet.

Jake followed her inside, closing the front door firmly behind him. He watched her steadily with his dark eyes as she turned to stare defiantly back at him.

"Well?"

"I came to update you on the progress made so far," he said easily.

Brianna wondered if that were true or only a trumped-up excuse. Wishful thinking on her part, no doubt. Jake had never had to trump up anything.

"I thought Officer Winston was the one in charge of this investigation." She sat down on a chair in the living room, gesturing to another for Jake.

He took the offered chair. Brianna noticed he didn't remove his heavy coat. He was obviously not planning to stay long.

"Don's in charge. But he filled me in and I told him I'd be seeing you and could let you know."

"Why?" she asked again.

"Why what?"

"Why bother? Officer Winston could have done the job. I think you've made it abundantly clear we have nothing to say to each other. So why were you the one to come by? Especially when a phone call would have sufficed."

He ran his fingers through his hair and leaned forward, wanting to shake her for being so elusive, for being so darn pretty sitting there practically ordering him out of her house.

He wanted to rail at her for shutting him out, for being all he could not have.

She'd invited him for dinner only a few hours ago; now she was as cool as the snow in the yard, as distant as summer.

"We talked to the duty officer at the base and obtained a list of people who had an idea of what projects you worked on. We cross-checked with the university. Got another list. We've been investigating the names on each list to see if anyone needed quick cash and consequently might be interested in minor espionage. We're trying to determine who knew you had access to classified files, and that you'd be away for a week at Christmas."

"Good grief, you're questioning all my friends?" she asked in disbelief. "Why don't you put an ad in the paper? Anyone who knows Brianna Hart come forward and be suspected of—"

"It's routine police work and so far has resulted in nothing. But I wanted you to know we're doing all we can to make sure we catch the man."

"A telephone call would have worked."

He had just come by to update her on the investigation. She didn't know why he'd kissed her, but she'd bet her last dollar he hadn't expected her to respond so fervently. She'd all but plastered herself to him. She wanted to melt into a puddle of embarrassment. But she held on. She wouldn't give way until he left.

"I wanted to see you," he admitted.

"That wasn't the impression I got this morning on the phone." She looked away, remembering how hurt she'd felt at his rejection.

"Yeah, well, the reason I didn't want to come to dinner is I didn't want a scene like we just had on your front walk. There's no future in it." That much he did know.

What's wrong with me that you can't love me? she screamed inside. Gritting her teeth hard, she clamped down on the words.

"Have you seen anyone suspicious around here or around your office?"

"Officer Winston asked me that. No, I haven't. And I'll be sure to let him know if I do."

"Him, not me?" Jake asked, his voice whipcord sharp.

"He's still in charge, isn't he?"

Leave, leave, leave, she willed him. Just leave me alone once and for all.

This was torture to be so close, to have shared hot kisses, and still hear him say they had no future together. What did he want from her?

Jake rose, towering over her. "Yes, he's the one in charge." Slowly he leaned over, his finger rubbing gently against her swollen lips. "I didn't hurt you, did I?"

She shook her head. *Not the way you mean.*

With an exasperated sigh, he straightened and turned to the door. "I can see myself out."

Brianna remained perfectly still. Her eyes watched him walk away. Her ears heard the door open, close. Her body felt the silence and stillness of her empty house. She was alone—again.

But Jake's scent still surrounded her. The heat he engendered still warmed her body. The tiny pulses of electricity his very touch brought still hovered against her skin. Closing her eyes, she imagined he was still there with her. She sighed. It was going to be a long night.

And so it proved. It was after midnight and still she couldn't fall asleep. Groaning in frustration she rolled onto her side. The scene between them earlier that evening replayed over and over in her mind.

She couldn't forget how wonderful it had been to be in Jake's arms again. The pleasure she'd received in his kisses, the touch of his hands against her face, his fingers threaded in her hair burned in her memory. She yearned for more.

Bother! At the rate she was going, she'd still be tossing and turning at dawn. She needed to get some sleep! She had a math section at eight in the morning, and those students were sharp. She needed to be on her toes to challenge them.

Flinging off her covers, she quickly rose. Maybe some cocoa or a brandy or something would relax her enough to fall asleep. What she really needed was to get her mind off Jake. But that didn't look likely in the next few centuries.

She padded silently down the short hall and reached

the door to the kitchen at the same instant the window glass broke. Startled at the sound, she snapped on the switch by the door, flooding in the scene with revealing fluorescent light.

She caught a glimpse of a hand and arm, quickly yanked out of the window and then gone. Shock held her immobile for a long moment, then she flew to the phone to call the police.

As calmly as she could, she explained the situation to the dispatcher. He promised immediate help. Even as she hung up, she could hear the distant wail of a siren. Apprehensively she stayed by the phone, watching the kitchen door to see if anyone came through. She heard nothing but the blood pounding through her veins. She thought she'd scared the intruder away, but she wasn't sure. She yanked on her coat and stood by the front door, tense and alert. If anyone came in through the kitchen, she'd flee out the front.

Seconds later, heavy pounding shook the door. Brianna whipped it open and almost flung herself into the policeman's arms.

In less than half an hour, things were back to normal. The officer had temporarily patched the window, scoured the grounds for an intruder, written down her statement and posted a patrol to survey the neighborhood until morning.

The disturbance had awakened the Bensons, and when they heard what had happened, they insisted Brianna spend the rest of the night with them.

Gratefully she accepted. For one brief moment, she was tempted to call Jake. Gathering up her things, she locked the door behind her, wondering if she should consider moving. If these break-ins threatened to become a habit, she'd have to. She couldn't continue to live like this.

Snuggled down in the guest room of the Bensons' a few minutes later, Brianna seriously wondered what anyone could want badly enough to break into her house twice. She had no classified secrets, no final exams, no jewelry. It was most puzzling. Reading mysteries was fun, this not so much.

Immediately following that thought came the speculation about what Jake would do when he heard about this night's adventure. She really didn't need his help. The other police officers in the city were all competent individuals. And a lot less threatening to her own stable well-being.

He'd mentioned again last night that they had no future together. She'd do nothing but set herself up for a load of heartache if she continued to see him, no matter how she longed to do so.

Starting tomorrow morning, she'd stand on her own two feet again. And if she needed some help, she'd call one of her brothers. They'd be here like a shot.

With that resolution firmly fixed in her mind, she finally drifted off to sleep.

Her home looked the same the next morning when she returned to dress for school. Officer Winston caught her right before she left for campus. He reviewed the report the duty officers had prepared and asked a few more questions.

"I'm not sure how safe it is for you to remain here

by yourself. Do you have another place you can stay until we can find the intruder? Someone like a close friend or relative?" he queried as he prepared to leave.

"Do you really think I'm in some sort of danger?" Brianna asked.

"The perpetrator had to know you were home last night. That makes the entire situation more dangerous. It seems as if our guy is getting more desperate."

She nodded, still baffled by what anyone could want from her. "I have some friends I could stay with I guess. I can't move in with someone indefinitely."

"We'll see if we can get any leads from last night's attempt. Until then, Miss Hart, I'd suggest you find another place to stay for the next few nights at least."

The interview with Officer Winston made her late. And Thursdays were her heavy days. She dashed from the parking lot to her first class, feeling as if she was out of step with the rest of the world.

The feeling lasted through the morning. Without the calm preparation time she usually enjoyed, it seemed as though she was constantly scrambling to catch up. And always at the back of her mind was the constant worry about the break-ins.

Grabbing a quick lunch, she wondered which of her friends she should ask for a favor. Sandy would be the best bet, not having any family to disrupt.

Her brother Josh lived too far away, plus he still acted as if she were a baby.

She liked being independent. She didn't want to be under his overprotective thumb again. Yet Brianna wondered if leaving her place unattended would offer an open invitation to the intruder to try again.

What did he want?

Brianna's last class of the day was advanced calculus for mathematics majors. She was well into the lecture, turning from writing a complex formula on the blackboard, when her eye caught the opening of the back door. Jake Morgan walked into the lecture hall and went to stand against the back wall. Brianna swallowed hard, losing her train of thought for a moment.

What was he doing here?

She caught sight of the puzzled faces of the students, several of whom had turned to see what was causing her momentary distraction. Taking a deep breath, Brianna picked up the threads of her lecture and plunged in again. Feeling more vibrantly alive than just seconds before, she was aware of Jake's steady regard while she wrapped up the lecture for the day.

What was he doing here, and dressed as he was? He leaned negligently against the wall, wearing all black, from the dark boots and black cords to the thick black sweater that hugged his torso. He tossed a shearling jacket over the back of a seat, crossed his strong arms over his muscular chest and stared at her.

Brianna could scarcely concentrate. He was far too distracting.

She wanted to discuss some theorems, but couldn't remember which ones. She wanted to excite her students with the knowledge of the practical uses of calculus, but could only feel the excitement that being near Jake brought.

Finally, unable to concentrate, she dismissed the

class ten minutes early. From the eager sounds from the students, she'd made their day.

Slowly the lecture hall emptied until only Jake and Brianna remained. She busied herself stacking the assignments that had been turned in and erasing the blackboard. Aware that Jake remained leaning against that back wall, studying her, she did her best to ignore him.

When the last student vanished, Jake pushed away from the wall and walked down the side of the room, his step measured and soft. Brianna was resigned to watch him approach, her heart beating double time.

His dark eyes almost shot flames as they narrowed in on hers and held them captive. A muscle in his cheek jumped as he clenched his teeth. His broad shoulders were displayed to advantage in the dark sweater. The black cords encased long, muscular legs.

Her gaze dropped to his lips. Involuntarily she licked her own, wanting to feel his against hers one more time. How many one-more-times were there in life?

Never enough, she was sure.

He stopped close to her, so close she could feel his body heat brush against her own, could see the thick lashes that framed his dark eyes, could smell the tangy masculine scent that was his alone. The scent that she would recognize anywhere, anytime. Something melted deep within her and she took a step closer.

She was like a moth attracted to flame. She knew she'd get burned, but she couldn't help herself. She had to touch that heat.

"You're in big trouble, little lady," he growled.

Exhilaration spread to every cell in her body as his rough voice caressed her senses. Challenged, she flashed a haughty look and poked his chest with her forefinger.

"I'm not a little lady. I'm five foot nine."

He captured the finger and drew it to his mouth. Nipping it gently, he soothed the tip with his tongue. Brianna's legs grew wobbly. Slowly she inched closer to brace herself against his greater strength.

"From six-five you're not so big." He planted a hot, damp kiss in the palm of her hand, his fingers lacing with hers as he let their hands drop. Bringing them up behind her, he urged her the last few inches until her breasts pressed against his chest, her belly snuggled against his, her thighs felt the strength of his.

"But definitely a lady." Leaning over, he brushed his lips light against hers.

"Jake, you can't just come into my classroom like this and disrupt everything."

"Excuse me, Teacher, but I merely walked in and stood in the rear. I never said a word." His free hand wandered up to encircle her neck, his fingers gentle against her nape. His other arched her more firmly against him, holding her a willing captive.

"I..."

It was true. He'd done nothing but show up. All the disruption had been caused by her own reaction to seeing him.

She was having trouble thinking. Pressed up against him so intimately, she was having trouble even breathing, let alone coming up with the fortitude to push him away.

His hand tilted her jaw, exposing her throat. With a

soft groan, he lowered his mouth to that silky skin, kissing her, licking her, blowing gently on the damp skin. He was seducing her in her own classroom!

Brianna shivered and shifted even closer, her free hand surrounding his waist, slipping beneath his sweater to press against his hot skin. Her breasts tingled with desire; heat pooled deep within her. Her legs remained wobbly, unable to support her weight.

"Why didn't you call me last night?" he asked.

She blinked, tried to back away, but was caught fast by his arm.

"I told you to call me if anything happened. How do you think I felt hearing from Don this morning that there'd been another break-in? And this one happened when you were there!"

"There's no need for you to get involved."

Disappointment raged through her. Had he only come because of last night's attempted break-in, out of some overextended sense of duty?

"Besides, there wasn't anything you could have done that the policeman on duty last night didn't do. I spent the rest of the night with the Bensons."

"I sure as hell could have done something. Exactly what I'm going to do now," he said, releasing her and turning to the lecture desk. "This all your stuff?"

The sudden change was unexpected. Brianna nodded.

"Where do you want it?" He gathered up the stack of papers and folders.

"In my office, but I can manage."

She reached for them, but he was already heading

toward the back of the hall. Snagging his jacket en route, he waited for her by the door.

"Jake, I can manage," she repeated.

"Sure, you've done a great job so far. Let's go. We've got a long ride ahead of us."

"What are you talking about?" She almost had to skip to keep up with his longer stride. Throwing on her coat, she dodged a group of students and followed him from the lecture hall to her office.

He dumped her papers on her desk and turned to take her arm. "Let's go."

She dug in her heels and pulled Jake to a stop.

"Wait a darn minute. Just what do you think you're doing? And where do you think we're going?"

"I'm taking you out of Texarkana for a couple of days. It's too dangerous for you to stay around while some crook keeps breaking into your house."

"I'm not going with you. I was going to stay with Sandy for a couple of days—"

"Yeah, Don told me he had you arrange to stay somewhere else. Call and cancel."

"I haven't arranged it yet, but I—"

"Good, then there's no problem. Need anything from here?"

"Hold it! I'm not going anywhere with you."

Her mind boggled at the notion. Spend several days alone with Jake, no one else around? No matter how much the idea appealed, it would be emotional suicide. Yet a tiny portion of her couldn't resist just hearing what he had to say. Nothing more.

"Where?" she asked.

That slow, seductive smile he gave so sparingly tilted the corners of his lips. Her heart caught fire. She'd walk through fire for those smiles.

"I have a place up in the Winding Stairs Mountains a couple of hours from here. We'll stay the weekend there. That'll give Don and his men a chance to follow up on some leads and stake out your house without your being around."

"What leads?"

"We caught a break. You have a new mama in your complex. She'd just put baby to sleep when she heard the breaking glass. She looked out the window and caught a glimpse of the intruder. She was even able to give us a partial description of his car. We'll get him, Brie. We just need time."

"Then I'll be fine at home."

"Until then, you're coming with me."

He tugged gently and she went with him. Her thoughts churning, Brianna tried to decide the best course of action. The *prudent* course of action, not what her heart clamored for.

"We can't leave for the weekend. It's only Thursday," she protested, trying frantically to come up with convincing reasons his plan would never work. She had to be calm and rational about it all and come up with a sound reason to stay as far from him as possible.

"That was your last class, wasn't it?"

"Yes. What about your work?"

"I'm taking a few days' vacation. I haven't had one in years so they owe me."

She was intrigued. "Why not?"

"Why not what?" He glanced down at her as they reached his car. "Will your car be all right here over the weekend?"

She looked around. "If I were leaving it here for the weekend, it would be, but—"

"Get into the car." He hustled her into his four-wheel-drive Jeep, leaned so close she thought he was going to kiss her again.

"I'm not sure this is such a good idea," she whispered.

"I'll keep you safe," he promised.

"Will you?"

He hadn't before. She'd been so hurt. And he didn't even have a clue. It was probably a good thing he didn't know how he affected her. Could she stand to have her heart broken a second time?

Forty-five minutes later, they were heading toward Oklahoma. Two suitcases in the back seat contained their clothes. Brianna had her briefcase containing two journals she wanted to read, but Jake had refused to let her take any other work.

They were well beyond the city limits before Brianna allowed the enormity of the situation to hit her fully. She was going away for the weekend with the man she loved.

Yet from his point of view, he was merely protecting her from an unknown intruder. When the man was caught, Jake would say goodbye and she'd once again be on her own.

Until then—she had three days at least, maybe more. She could store up a lifetime of memories in three days. She'd have to. It was unlikely an opportunity like this would come again.

Smiling suddenly, she knew she could have resisted. She had other options. Jase would come stay with her. Josh would have had her at the ranch. It wasn't that long a drive into Texarkana from the ranch that she couldn't have done it every day for a while. Or she could have stayed with Sandy.

The real reason she agreed to Jake's demands to go with him was that she wanted to. It was that simple.

This time she knew there was no future for them. She was no longer the starry-eyed woman who had believed in happy endings. She wouldn't be caught unaware as she had been two years ago when he stopped calling. Now she knew she'd have to save up memories and be prepared to say goodbye when they returned.

Four

The sparkling snow reflected the sun's rays until Brianna wondered how Jake could see to drive. She donned dark glasses and looked out the side window. The fields along the road were pristine and empty beneath their snowy covering. In the distance, she saw a small herd of cattle, but they had not trampled the snow near the road. For a moment, she was transported back to her childhood. She and her brothers had loved the snow, made snow angels, built forts, had rousing snowball fights. As the youngest, she'd rarely won the snowball fights, but she never stopped trying.

She tried to remember the last snowball fight. It had to be just before her parents had been killed. It seemed as if Jase had changed overnight after that.

Of course, he would have had to. He'd been responsible for her and Josh.

Funny, she'd never thought about it much before. How hard that must have been for him. He'd only been a kid himself.

"Worried about something?" Jake asked with a quick glance in her direction.

She turned, jolted back to the present. "No, just

remembering when I was a kid and the fun my brothers and I had in the snow. Doesn't seeing all this make you want to get out and play?"

He shrugged. "I like some things in the snow. Skiing, snowmobiling. What do you mean by play?"

"Play in the snow itself. I loved making snow angels when I was little. My mom would come out and judge whose were the best. I always won." Brianna smiled in reminiscence. "Maybe because it was the only thing I could win. My brothers never gave an inch. And since they're both older, I didn't have a chance."

"They watch out for you," he said neutrally.

"Well, Jase sure did. He worked hard to keep me and Josh with him after my folks died. But Josh, too, started bossing me around after Mom and Dad were gone. Guess they took their responsibilities very seriously."

"Jase is your older brother, right?"

"Yes. He was just a kid himself when Mom and Dad died. The judge waited until he was eighteen and then granted him custody of us until we came of age. But Josh was bossier."

Jake darted her a quick glance and remained silent. He said nothing. He knew how bossy her brother was, and how strongly Josh felt about protecting his sister.

Jake almost gave in to the temptation to tell her, as well, but the urge passed. It was old news. And Josh hadn't said anything untrue. Jake wasn't the man for Brianna. Josh had made that clear, but it would not have influenced Jake a bit if he hadn't agreed with the man. He had known Brianna had a crush on him. He had relished feeling special to such a warm and loving woman. But his way of life wasn't suitable for such a gentle woman, nor his background. She deserved much more. And Josh had known it.

"…sisters?" she said.

"What?" He'd missed the first part of her question while brooding on what had happened two years ago.

"I asked if you had any brothers or sisters? You never mentioned any when…before. But that doesn't mean you don't have any."

"I don't." His reply was clipped. He didn't want to talk about families.

Brianna studied Jake as he drove. He seemed lost in thought. When they'd been dating, he had sometimes been preoccupied, usually with a case he was working on. At that time, she'd felt comfortable enough to ask what he was thinking.

Not now. She longed to know what he'd been doing the past two years. She wondered about the crimes he'd investigated. She didn't even know what division he worked in, though she suspected burglary since he seemed to know all about her case.

More than anything, she wondered what he thought they'd accomplish by leaving Texarkana for a long weekend. Was it merely to keep her safe while the rest of the force searched for the burglar? Or was there more to it?

"I missed you these past years," she said bravely. "Did you miss me?"

He nodded once, briefly.

Her throat ached as she held back the words demanding to know why he'd stopped calling, why he hadn't responded to her calls.

"Where exactly are we going?" she asked instead.

"My place."

"I didn't know you had a place in the mountains. Where?"

"Not too far from the state park. I've had the land for a long time. A couple of summers ago, I built a small cabin. Some of the guys from work helped. Now I let them use it when I'm not coming up."

"I can't wait to see it."

"It's not much, just a couple of rooms. But the view's nice."

He was proud of the cabin. It wasn't much, but it was all his. He'd designed it, built it with help, and furnished it. He'd spent a couple of weeks right after it was built just sitting on the porch and staring at the view. Building it helped him forget about Brianna.

Sitting on the porch gave him unlimited time to remember her.

It was growing dark when he turned onto the narrow road leading to his place. Five minutes later, he pulled to a halt before a small log cabin. The wide front porch was well sheltered from the snow, which drifted considerably deeper in the yard than it had back in Texarkana.

At least it wasn't too deep he couldn't pull into the small drive.

Brianna's eyes darted everywhere as she took in the building, then the fantastic view.

"Jake, this is beautiful." Her voice was hushed as she gazed in delight at the scene. "You must come up here every chance you get."

"I don't get up that much." Building it had been a way to keep the memories at bay. But once he had completed the work, staying at the cabin proved lonely. It reminded him too much of things that he couldn't have.

Brianna hopped out of the car, glad she'd worn warm boots when she sank to her knees in the snow. Reaching for her briefcase, she turned and trudged to the porch. Jake followed, carrying both their bags.

Nestled in the lee of the mountains to the west, the cabin was already in shadow. Dusk would follow shortly. Opening the door, Jake stood aside as Brianna stepped inside. She looked everywhere, curious to see how he'd decorated it. It was Spartan, the furniture sturdy and practical and looked imminently comfortable. To the left of the doorway, she saw a long sofa placed in front of a stone fireplace with a couple of easy chairs flanking it. To the right, a large, scarred pine dining table sat surrounded by wooden chairs. Beyond was the open kitchen. A closed door split the back wall.

There were no curtains, no rugs, nothing to soften the stark lines. And nothing on the windows to interfere with the spectacular view.

Brianna itched to bring a little color to the room, to warm it up with curtains flanking the windows, comfortable pillows piled on the sofa, and a thick rug on the floor.

But it wasn't her place to do so.

Neither, apparently, was it any other woman's place. For that she was grateful.

"It's wonderful," she said, smiling at him.

He looked around the room as if seeing it for the first time and shook his head. In comparison to the warmth and color of her place, it was barren, almost bleak.

"Still not finished. But I'm not much on curtains and such. Maybe you have some suggestions." He closed the door and deposited their cases beside it. "I'll get a fire going. That's the primary method of heat. Don't take off your jacket just yet."

As Jake moved to the fireplace, Brianna dropped her briefcase on the sofa and went to gaze at the view through the front window. The cabin sat on the slope of a hill, with a small valley beneath it. The sunlight still shone on the opposite hill, the snow reflecting the late-afternoon colors of gold and pink. The worries about the break-ins seemed surreal in such a serene setting.

Brianna sighed with pleasure and turned to watch Jake build their fire.

"You could almost commute from here," she observed, perching on the arm of the sofa. The trip had taken only a couple of hours.

"No, I need to live in town. If I'm needed, I want to be right there. This is fine for weekends and vacations."

"Yet you said you don't come very often. Why not? I'd think you would come up all the time and bring loads of friends with you."

"It's not big enough for loads of friends."

"Then a special friend," she said as if probing a sore tooth.

He looked up and met her gaze. Slowly he stood, his eyes never leaving hers.

"I've never brought another woman, if that is what you're hinting at," he said pointedly.

Pink washed up through her cheeks as he answered her not-so-subtle question. She should have been embarrassed, but her relief that he did not habitually bring up other women was too strong. She was the first!

She wished she had had a hand in building it. Dare she take him up on his request to help decorate it?

She cleared her throat. "Why not?" she whispered.

He smiled and stepped closer. "There is only one bedroom." Reaching out his hand, he rubbed the back of his fingers over a heated cheek.

Her eyes widened at that. Did that mean…?

"Fortunately, the sofa opens out to a bed." Teasing lights danced in his eyes as he studied the myriad expressions dancing across her face.

She wished she were as brazen as she sometimes was in her dreams. She'd love to be bold enough to step into his arms and say not to bother with the sofa bed, there'd be plenty of room in his bed for both of them.

But while wanton fantasies were fine for dream time, they didn't have a place in real life.

He dropped his hand and shrugged out of his jacket.

The fire had started, and already Brianna could feel some of its warmth.

"There are things in the freezer and cupboards. Let's see if we can find enough for dinner or if I have to go back out for some food."

Brianna trailed after Jake, shivering a little in the cold cabin, the temperature almost matching that of outside.

How long before it warmed up enough to be comfortable? With the fire, the stove and the oven, it should be toasty warm quickly.

She knew a shortcut. If he'd just kiss her once…

Even thinking about a kiss warmed her ten degrees. She unbuttoned her jacket and let it hang open.

Her eyes tracked Jake as he rummaged around in the cupboards and pulled out some cans and boxes. Then he moved to the freezer and searched through the frozen packages. Curling her fingers, she shoved her hands into her pockets to keep from acting on the urge to thread her fingers through his thick, dark hair. She spun around and gazed out the window over the sink, lest every private longing be revealed when he looked at her.

"That's it. Frozen steaks, boxed potatoes, canned corn." He looked up, a trace of uncertainty in his eyes.

Brianna met his gaze, touched. Was he worried about what she thought about dinner? She smiled.

"I can pan fry the steaks, make gravy and biscuits to go with it," she offered, turning to take off her jacket.

He was right there, easing the thick coat from her shoulders, tossing it across a chair, raising her chin with the edge of his hand.

"I remember your gravy and biscuits. They were always great."

"I'm glad you liked them. Men are so easy to please. Cook them a hearty meal, plenty of everything, and presto, instant satisfaction." She smiled saucily up at him. Feeling alive for the first time in two years, it was glorious.

"I remember you saying that once before, when we

had that barbecue." He hesitated a moment, then murmured, "I remember every word you said." His eyes searched hers, roaming over her face as if memorizing her features.

Brianna was struck dumb. *He remembered everything she'd said?* Then why—

"And I remember how mouth-watering good your cooking was. So I'm accepting that offer before you change your mind. There's another fireplace in the bedroom. I'll build a fire there so the room will be warm when you go to sleep tonight."

"I'll take the sofa," she said.

"You're my guest. You get the bed." He strode from the room before she could muster any arguments.

Brianna turned to the counter and began to prepare for dinner. She didn't really mind sleeping in his bed. It would probably be the only time she'd get the chance.

She was in the midst of cooking when Jake returned. She put him to work cutting out the biscuits and placing them on the baking sheet. While she kept a careful eye on the gravy, he whipped the potatoes. They worked well together, almost as if they'd worked in harmony for years.

Moving around each other as they performed their tasks, Brianna felt as if she were participating in an intricate dance. She and Jake passed, reached around each other and sidestepped out of the way, each time drawing closer and closer. Once she stopped dead and he bumped into her, carrying a bottle of wine and two glasses. If her hands hadn't been full of plates and forks, she would have reached up to touch his cheek. He stood so close his breath caressed her cheeks.

"You must be warm enough. There's color in your cheeks and your eyes are bright blue," he murmured, refusing to move. She had stepped in his way deliberately. If she didn't want to be there, she could step around him.

"It's the heat from the stove. Though the room seems to be warming up."

She leaned ever so slightly forward. Deliberately she ran her tongue over her lip and dared him to ignore her.

"If we do this very carefully, neither one of us will drop anything," he said, encircling her with his arms, holding the wine bottle so it didn't spill. The empty wineglasses clinked gently as his arms drew her in and his face lowered to hers.

His lips were warm and firm, moving across hers in a lover's caress.

Brianna sighed as she melted into his embrace, afraid to drop plates yet unwilling to step away. She savored his touch assailed by tremors that consumed her. She'd lived in a desert of emotions for so long. The glorious feelings that shimmered through her were thirst-quenching.

She'd never known such love before and knew she would never again experience this with another. Jake was the only man for her. She wasn't sure what had gone wrong between them, but it had nothing to do with this. Nothing could compare. In this they were as compatible as two people could ever be.

Slowly he raised his head ending the kiss.

Brianna was pleased to note his breathing was as erratic as hers. At least she wasn't the only one feeling something. Could she get him to admit as much? Get him to explain why he'd dropped her? Get him to consider some kind of relationship with her now?

"Is the meat burning?" he asked.

"Oh!" She whirled and slammed the plates on the counter, then snatched up the pan and pulled it from the stove. Great! Just when she needed to make a good impression, she scorched the steaks. Gingerly lifting the edge with a fork, she noted it was only slightly scorched. Salvageable, at least.

Was her relationship with Jake equally salvageable?

In short order, they set the table and she served dinner. Jake ate as if he hadn't eaten in a month, steadily, without talking.

"Were you that hungry?" she asked at one point. He could put away as much food as either of her brothers.

"I was hungry, but more for your cooking than anything else. I get tired of eating out or eating my own attempts."

She toyed with her wineglass, the deep red burgundy reflecting the flickering firelight.

"So what have you been doing these past couple of years?" she finally dared to ask. Heart pounding, she hoped he wouldn't refuse to answer. She longed to know everything he'd done, everyone he'd met, every place he'd gone.

"Working mostly. Built this place."

"But no vacations."

He shrugged. "I took time off to build this." And he'd been glad to have this project. "Though I know it doesn't look finished. Any ideas about curtains and things?" he asked.

She glanced around the large, open room. "I could make some suggestions. Don't you have someone else you would rather have a hand in this?" What of Diane? she wanted to ask. Just who is that woman and what's she to you?

"Your house is a good example of what I'd like. It's—welcoming, I guess is the best way to describe it."

She smiled, pleased he liked her home. She'd spent a lot of time fixing it up to suit her. She hadn't had much else to do.

"A weekend doesn't offer enough time to do a lot, but I'll think about it and try to come up with some ideas," she said.

"Decide what you think it needs. Next week I can go shopping and bring everything out next time I come," he said.

Her heartbeat sped up. He planned to go shopping, maybe she could suggest she go with him. And come back when he did to see how everything looked once curtains were up, rugs laid out and pillows tossed on the sofa.

"Okay." She could scarcely contain her excitement at her idea. Now to convince him.

"I could help with the shopping, too," she offered.

He looked at her for a moment, then shrugged. "We'll see."

She knew better than to push the issue.

There was time enough if she was spending the next couple of days here.

As recently as her drive back from Jase and

Shannon's, she'd never expected to see Jake again. She'd been reminded this past Christmas of all she was missing when in the presence of her older brother and his petite wife. Now that they had a baby on the way, Brianna was even more envious.

Jake and Brianna did the dishes companionably; she washed while he dried and put away. It didn't take long for the two of them to finish. When he handed her the dishtowel to dry her hands, she grabbed each end and tossed the towel over his head, pulling him toward her. His arms went easily around her as if they had been embracing for years.

"What do you want?" he asked huskily, backing her against the counter, holding her securely in his arms.

She opened her mouth to tell him exactly what she wanted, what she had wanted for two years, but nothing came out. Heat stole up into her face, and butterflies danced in her stomach. She swallowed hard and squeaked out, "Coffee?"

"In front of the fire?" he asked, his voice low and sexy, his eyes dark and intense as he gazed down into her flushed face.

She nodded, her hands gripping the towel, resting against his solid chest. Held in his arms, she felt the tug of love as before.

He towered over her, an uncommon event in her life. Except for her brothers and one of the ranch hands on the family spread, Brianna usually met most men eye to eye.

"Do you still want sugar in it?" she asked, slowly releasing one end of the towel and pulling it from around his neck.

He nodded, releasing her. Taking one hand, he separated her fingers and held one up. "Just dip this in the cup and it'll sweeten it enough." Then he kissed the tip.

Brianna leaned against the counter, thankful for its support. Her legs felt like jelly, her heart thudded and heat engulfed her. It made the fire in the fireplace superfluous. Tears stung her eyes.

He'd said that so many times before. She'd forgotten. How could she have forgotten? It had been such a special joke between them.

"Hey, what's wrong?" he asked, one thumb rubbing just beneath her lashes, capturing a tear.

"Nothing, I just was remembering." She tried a wobbly smile. "You used to say that a lot."

"You were always the sweetest thing I ever knew," he said so softly she almost didn't hear him.

When Jake planted a damp kiss in the center of her palm, she instinctively closed her fingers over the spot, sheltering it. Turning on shaky legs, she reached for the coffee. His mouth grazed against her hair. He gently pushed it aside and she felt his lips brush her neck.

"You're making it somewhat difficult to concentrate," she said, her voice shaky. "Do you want coffee or not?"

For an endless moment, he didn't answer. She longed to turn and see his expression, but too afraid of what her own might reveal, she refrained.

"Yes, I want coffee." So saying, he straightened and walked into the living room.

Brianna chanced a glance toward him as she poured the ground coffee into the filter. He added wood to the fire until it blazed. She felt the heat clear across the space. Her eyes moved to the bedroom. Was the fire in there as warm?

"I need to change the sheets," Jake said, standing and heading for the bedroom.

With a glance at the coffeemaker, Brianna headed for the bedroom, as well. It would be several minutes before the coffee finished brewing.

"I'll help."

The bedroom was almost as large as the living room. The windows reflected back their images of the night. It definitely required curtains.

Brianna didn't like feeling so exposed after all that had happened recently. The sooner he got curtains, at least for this room, the better, as far as she was concerned. Funny, before the incidents with the break-ins she hadn't minded an open window. Would she feel more comfortable once they'd caught the man?

Together they made the large bed. The headboard held reading lamps. She hoped he had some books. The journals she'd brought weren't the kind of reading she'd like if she slipped beneath the thick pile of covers, to read for a while, before going to sleep.

"The bathroom's through there. I should have told you earlier," Jake said, interrupting her thoughts and nodding toward the open door. "The hot water heater is propane. As you know from doing the dishes, we have plenty of hot water. You can take a bath or shower, if you wish."

"I'll wait until morning, if that's okay with you." Patting the pillow one last time, she skirted the bed and headed for the kitchen. Safety in distance right now, she thought, hoping she could resist the urge to throw herself into his arms and hold on tight until morning.

The delicious aroma of fresh coffee filled the cabin. Brianna poured their cups, added cream to hers and sugar to Jake's. Carrying the cups carefully to the sofa, she placed them within easy reach and sat down. It was cozy before the fire.

Drowsily she settled back and gazed into the dancing flames. She always liked staring into fires, watching the different images the flames suggested.

Jake came in and dumped a pile of bedding on one of the chairs. Sitting down beside her, he reached for his cup.

"This is nice. I don't have a fireplace in my house. That's one thing I really regret about it," she murmured, sipping from her cup.

"Cutting enough wood to last the winter can be a pain, but I think it's worth it every time I come," he said.

They sat quietly for a while, sipping coffee, watching the fire.

When Brianna finished hers, she placed the empty cup down on the floor. When she sat back up, Jake reached for her hand, threading his fingers through hers, resting their linked hands on his thigh. He continued to sip his coffee silently.

Brianna leaned back on the sofa, her only anchor to reality was her touch with Jake. Idly she daydreamed. She was full, warm, happy. For the first time in a long long time, she felt totally content.

"Tell me about your house." Jake broke the silence. "When did you buy it?"

"I bought it about eighteen months ago. As I said, I signed up for the part-time job at the air base and had enough money. I can use the tax break."

"I used to see you riding your bike sometimes if I was near the campus," he said lazily.

Turning her head on the back of the cushion, she looked at him. "When?" She hadn't seen him in two years. Yet he'd seen her?

"In the spring. One time during the summer."

"That's one advantage of the town house, its location. I can ride my bike to the college in nice weather. Even walk if I want to. I didn't see you."

"Unmarked car. I thought you'd be married by now."

Startled, she sat up and shook her head.

"Why would you think such a thing?" She pulled her hand away from his and sat on the edge of the sofa, looking at him.

Had her feelings for him been so nebulous to him that he thought she'd gone on to another man as soon as he was out of the picture? Had she seemed too intent for marriage? Was that the reason he'd pulled back?

He shrugged. "Just did."

Brianna tried to remember if she'd ever done anything to give him the feeling she was desperate for marriage. Two years ago, she'd only been twenty-four. Granted, she'd talked a lot about some of her friends who were getting married. Surely Jake hadn't thought she was trying to pin him down to popping the question.

Although if he'd asked her, she'd have accepted in a New York minute.

"I have no plans to marry," she said.

He put his cup on the floor, and turned to face her.

"That's not the way I heard it." Even now he could feel the anger rise. Josh had been blunt and frank. Jake had known even then that Josh was right. But it still hurt.

"I might marry one day. But I have no plans at the present. No prospects. I'm building my career." She didn't want to talk about marriage when the only one she had ever considered marrying didn't want her.

"You had plans two years ago," he persisted.

Now she thought she'd die of embarrassment. How had he learned of her foolish daydreams? Had she given herself away? For weeks she had dreamed of making a life with Jake. Had he known all along?

Rising, she scooped up the two cups and headed for the kitchen. "A lot of things have changed since then. I don't think my future plans concern you. Don't worry that I'll pester you once you find whoever's breaking into my place. I've managed fine on my own and will continue to do so."

She stormed into the kitchen, placing the cups in the sink with exaggerated care, afraid she might turn and smash them against the wall, so great was her embarrassment and frustration.

She should have called Sandy and insisted on staying with her. She knew she was playing with fire in coming with Jake, but she hadn't been able to resist. She hadn't expected him to bring up her foolish daydreams about marriage. She thought she had been the only one to know.

"Brie…" He followed her into the kitchen.

Glancing over her shoulder, she stepped to one side, giving him as wide a berth as she could.

"My name is Brianna. Only my family and close friends call me Brie," she lashed out, hurt and humiliated.

"Friends is what I thought we were. Until…"

Until you wanted more. If he had shouted the words, she could not have heard them more plainly.

"I'm tired. I'm going to bed. I'll be finished in the bathroom in a few minutes if you want to use it then," she said stiffly, heading for the bedroom.

She went straight into the bathroom, gritting her teeth to keep from crying. Be careful what you asked for, she repeated silently. You might get it and have it totally backfire. She couldn't wait to leave and return home— even if some crook was trying to break into her house. At the moment it seemed a better solution than staying here.

Jake leaned against the counter, crossing his arms over his chest, his eyes still on the closed bedroom door. What had happened? Obviously she was still hurting from the man who had deserted her.

He smiled mirthlessly. Hadn't her brother Josh been able to salvage the relationship once Jake had stepped out of the picture? That must have been frustrating for Josh. Josh had nothing on him in the frustration department!

She was as pretty as he remembered, maybe even prettier. He loved listening to her voice. How many nights had he laid in bed thinking about her? Even now, two years later, if he let himself, he'd storm in there and demand they try again.

Except, it wouldn't work any more now than before.

He turned and clicked off the lights. Sprawling out on the sofa, he watched the fire as it dwindled. He'd add some logs to last through the night before he went to sleep. But for now he listened to the quiet sounds from the bedroom and wished things had been different.

Five

By the time Brianna was ready to face Jake the next morning, she had herself firmly in hand. She hadn't slept well, but that was becoming a habit since she'd started seeing Jake again. Trying to live down her behavior of the previous day would prove a challenge. She decided as soon as she awoke that she wouldn't let herself forget for a single moment that she was here only because the police thought it safer than staying home.

There would be no more tossing a towel around Jake's neck and pulling his face down for a kiss. No more suggestive remarks leading to comments about her fingers being sweet as sugar. If he wanted coffee, he could get it himself. She'd focus on the real reason for her presence in his house and behave accordingly.

Brianna believed all the admonitions she'd given herself until she walked into the kitchen and saw Jake. Instantly, every thought flew from her head.

He wore only jeans.

She swallowed hard.

It wasn't fair. She'd had the best intentions in the world when she left the bedroom, but that was before she saw all that expanse of bare skin. His shoulders had always been broad. They gleamed, muscular and enticing, in the early sunlight that shone through the uncovered windows. The light dusting of dark hair on his chest looked silky. She longed to brush her fingers through it to ascertain exactly how soft it really was. The sleek muscles in his back bunched and flexed beneath his taut skin as he scooped coffee into the filter, stretched to fill the carafe with water.

She swallowed hard again, her eyes tracing over every mouth-watering inch, her fingertips tingling, heat rising.

"Aren't you cold?" she asked abruptly.

He needed to put on a shirt before she lost what tenuous control she held. When he turned, she knew she was done for.

He was gorgeous in the only way a perfect man can be. His hair was tousled, sexy as could be. His cheeks and chin bristled with day-old beard.

When had she developed this longing to rub against that stubborn jaw, to feel the scratchiness that covered the hard cheekbones? Such a compelling urge proved almost impossible to resist. She actually took a step closer before she caught herself.

"I'm not cold. I thought the fire had warmed the place up," he returned. "Are you cold?"

She was hotter than billy blue blazes, but it had nothing to do with the fire in the fireplace. The blame could be squarely laid at his feet. She glanced down. Even his feet were bare.

Closing her eyes, Brianna took a deep breath.

Opening them again, she forced her gaze to meet his. Ignoring the tempting expanse of male flesh only a few feet away was nothing short of miraculous. She was proud of herself.

"I'm not hot, but I am wearing more clothes than you." Blast! She had not meant for her voice to crack.

He looked at her oddly. "I was waiting my turn in the bathroom. I'll take a quick shower. There's not much for breakfast. Oatmeal, maybe?"

"That's fine."

"Are you all right?"

"Yes, why?" She couldn't breathe. How long could a person live without breathing?

"You look as if you're in a trance or something."

"I'm just looking you in the eye."

He frowned.

Sighing in defeat, Brianna let her gaze roam over the decidedly masculine body that stood before her. Slowly she licked her lips and stepped closer.

"You know, Jake, you probably should go get that shower now," she said, reaching out to touch his biceps. His skin was warm and taut. Lightly she skimmed her fingertip down his arm, feeling its silky texture change to the light roughness where darker hair covered his forearm.

"Yeah." But he didn't move. Then he did. Only to step closer, draw her up against that wide, enticing chest and lower his mouth to hers.

His scratchy beard abraded her softer cheeks, but she didn't care. She welcomed him, reaching for him. Her heart rate increased a hundredfold.

Brianna encircled his shoulders, her fingers, palms, arms, rubbing against the bare flesh that tantalized her so. Relishing in the sensations, she wanted the embrace to never end.

His mouth made love to hers as never before. He demanded and offered, took and returned. His hands cupped her head, holding her where he wanted her as he sipped from her lips, plunged again and again into the sweetness that waited for him.

When he lifted his head, Brianna wanted to rush outside and plunge into the nearest snow bank to cool the blazing heat that threatened to consume her. Her lips were warm—the air cooled them. Her body was hot—nothing cooled it. Locking her gaze with his, she refused to release him. Her arms had a mind of their own.

"I've got to take a shower," he said, his hands brushing through her soft hair. His eyes were distracted as he watched the silken locks drift over and over between his fingers as he continued to comb through.

"I'll make breakfast."

He smiled down at her, his eyes dark and shadowy. Nodding slowly, he lowered his head again. This time the kisses were feathery light. Just a touch of his lips against hers. Not nearly enough to assuage the burning need that threatened to overwhelm her.

Brianna stood on tiptoes to increase contact. He smiled against her, his lips moving over hers, yet denying her the full satisfaction she sought.

Remembering too late her own admonitions of only a few minutes ago, she pulled away. Clearing her throat, she tried for a reasonable tone. Shimmering waves of excitement tingled through her. Reasonable was not at all how she felt.

"Go." She stepped around him and stared at the coffee, trying to drag her raging emotions under some semblance of control. She'd never make it through the weekend if she didn't maintain some decorum.

Though who wanted decorum when they could have Jake served up practically naked first thing in the morning?

It was like playing house, she decided a little later as the sound of the shower ended.

They had never even spent the night together before this weekend. Now they were living together. Not in the full sense of the word, but close enough to know how it would be.

And as far as she was concerned, it would be great. They got along. They had some interests in common, and some different. But in the past, and during the last two days, they'd spent endless hours together without any cross words. And she had never been bored around him.

Could he say the same?

A thought struck her. Did she bore him? That could explain—

"Is this a new thing with you, going off into a trance?" Jake asked, walking into the room.

She spun around. He'd dressed. He wore faded jeans and another dark sweater. He had on black socks, no shoes yet.

"I was just thinking. Do I bore you?"

"What?" He looked startled. Shaking his head, he

chuckled. "Honey, the last thing you could ever do is bore me. I can't keep up with you. Where did that notion come from?"

"I was thinking that you don't bore me and I wondered if I bored you. Do you like brown sugar on your oatmeal or cinnamon?"

"Sugar, of course. You've never come close to boring me, Brie."

She dished up breakfast and watched him from beneath veiled lashes as he ate. She liked playing house.

"I thought we could take out the snowmobiles after we ate," Jake said as he poured himself a mug of coffee.

"That would be fun."

"You've ridden snowmobiles before?"

"Sure. We have several at the ranch. Sometimes Josh and Jase use them instead of horses to reach some of the outlying ranges to check cattle if there's snow on the ground. I've ridden them many times when I went along to help."

"Good. We'll ride when we finish eating. We can go down to the convenience shop and get some food for the rest of the weekend."

"Okay."

Spending the morning in the cold air and snow would be the best thing for her. Get her mind off Jake.

Then when they got back, she would read her journals, maybe make soup or something time-consuming for dinner.

She had three days to get through before they'd head for home. She had to find things to keep her busy or go crazy.

Snowmobiling provided a perfect solution. Cold and windy, the crisp morning proved a total antidote to the heat that had suffused her. Glad for the change from the cabin, she snuggled down in her parka, knowing she'd warm up as they traveled.

Following Jake, Brianna was able to keep up with no trouble. And she got to watch him to her heart's content. As he led the way, it took only a couple of minutes before she knew she was in the presence of an expert. On her mettle to prove her own ability, she followed right behind him. If he could do it, so could she.

It was exhilarating! The swirl of snow that shot from beneath the traces spun like sugar in the bright sun. Rainbows and dazzling sparklers reflected back the variety of crystalline snowflakes. The sky was so blue it almost hurt. The air was so clean and clear it seemed almost as if she were breathing pure oxygen. She laughed aloud in sheer happiness.

They reached the convenience store only a few miles down the road and left the snowmobiles neatly parked beside the larger cars. She giggled at the picture their two vehicles made.

Jake snatched off her cap and watched as she shook her head free in the frosty air. "Your hair is just as blond in winter as in summer," he said, handing her the cap.

"That's because it's still sun-bleached. I don't wear a hat when I ski so the sun can still get to it."

Pleased he commented on it, she wanted him to notice every single thing about her. Something would click. She couldn't be the only one to feel so strongly in this relationship.

When Jake scanned the area before heading for the store, Brianna shivered. Instantly she was reminded why they were there. He looked like a cop now. All business. He had her with him to guard her, to make sure she remained unharmed. It was easier to forget when it was just the two of them, but being in a public place brought it all up again.

"Jake, I'm not being stalked. Someone broke into my house and office," she said, stepping closer. No matter what, she felt safer near him.

"Old habits die hard. Come on, what do you want for dinner tonight?"

He took a different route back to the cabin, passing a couple of places that afforded a magnificent view of the snow-covered hills and valleys. One spot offered a spectacular panorama of the Winding Stairs summit in all its winter beauty.

The groceries had not yet been put away when Jake's cell rang. Jake answered. He glanced at Brianna, turned slightly and kept his comments brief. Brianna continued storing the food they'd just bought, shifting the supplies around in the cupboards. She listened with half an ear, but was unable to make heads or tails of the conversation from his cryptic comments.

Did it concern her? Had they found the person who had broken into her home?

When he put his phone back in his pocket, his face was grim.

The call reminded him why Brianna was there. It wasn't a romantic weekend getaway. He was keeping her safe from danger. And he'd better remember that.

"What now?" she asked.

"Someone broke into your car. The campus police called it in this morning. Don's keeping me informed."

"I shouldn't have left it at the college." Her legs felt shaky. Weakly she drew out a dining room chair and plopped down on the hard seat. "Is it a total mess like everything else?"

"The passenger window's broken. Nothing taken that they could tell."

Jake whipped out the chair next to hers, turned it around and straddled it, stacking his hands on the high back. He rested his chin on them and studied her.

"Maybe we've been going at this wrong, Brie. We need to find out who is doing this and why. I thought you must have something someone wants. But what would you have in your car? Now I wonder if it's just someone targeting you for some reason. Have you made anyone angry recently?"

She shook her head.

"How about not so recently, like a year or two ago, but for some reason they're only getting back at you now?"

Was it possible *she* had ended that other relationship? Was that the reason for the break-ins—retaliation by a rejected lover?

She shook her head.

"There has to be something!"

"Well, I don't know what it is! I'm not working on a project for the Air Force right now. I don't leave anything at home or at my office about that work ever. The new semester has just started, so I don't have any tests or exams around that a student might be trying to see."

"The fall semester ended when?"

"We had finals right before Christmas."

"Could it be a student looking for grades?"

She shrugged. "At this point I don't know who it could be. But I turned in my grades before I left for Jase and Shannon's place at Christmas."

"Would students know that? Could it be that simple?"

"Simple or not, I want it stopped. Why would they look in my car? I certainly wouldn't keep anything important in my car."

"Whoever it is, he took care to sweep away all the glass. If someone hadn't walked right by it and noticed the window was open, it might not have been discovered until you returned. No one leaves their windows open in this kind of weather."

"So he's been to my house twice, my office once and now my car. Should I leave a sign around that I don't have whatever it is he's looking for?"

"Tell me about the men in your life." He didn't want to hear what she had to say, but if it provided a clue, he needed to know.

The change was abrupt. She stared at Jake. Gone was the laughing rider on the snowmobile. Instead, she viewed a hard-eyed cop, intent on discovering any and all facts he could to solve a crime.

She wondered if she were still a person to him or had she become just another case?

"There are no men in my life," she said evenly.

"Come on, Brie, not so. You're too pretty to be alone. Who have you been dating recently? Who do you go out with for coffee after work? What student has a crush on you?"

The last thing she planned to do was let this man know how his leaving had impacted her life. She simply would not open herself up to that. Tilting her chin, she glared at him.

"First, I don't have any students who have crushes on me. Not that I know about. Wouldn't I be able to tell?"

He shook his head slowly. "I don't know. They might love you from afar."

"Right. Next, I have a friendly relationship with others in the mathematics department. But no one there is pining away over me. It may have escaped your attention, but I am no femme fatale."

"Honey, you're as pretty as the sunrise, as I'm sure you've been told many times. What you might view as only friendship, another might wish to change."

As she had with Jake. He'd considered them friends when she had wanted so much more.

"Give me something! I'm trying to help you here and you're as closed mouthed as a clam. Tell me what I need to know!"

She stood up and put her fists on her hips.

"I've told you everything I know. No one has a crush on me. I have no secrets at home. There is no man out there wreaking havoc in my life to get back at me for some imagined wrong. How many ways do I have to tell you that? I think it must be some deranged maniac targeting me for who-knows-what reason. But I don't know what it is, so stop asking me!"

She turned and stomped into the bedroom, slamming the door behind her. Her emotions were raw. She was a quivering mass of contradictions. She had begun to patch together her life after Jake had walked away so abruptly. Being around him now was no picnic.

She wanted him as much as she had before, if not more. And the vibes she got from him were so confusing. One minute she began to think he cared. Kisses were magical. The next she thought she represented nothing more to him than a challenging case for the great police detective to crack.

Flinging herself down on the bed, she frowned at the ceiling. Not six hours ago, she'd told herself she'd keep her distance from him. She refused to fall into the trap of believing there could be anything between them. She needed to remember Jake had made his feelings in the matter perfectly clear. Why then did she have such a hard time accepting them?

The bedroom door swung open. Brianna glanced over to the doorway. Jake leaned against the jamb, his arms crossed over his chest.

"Don't sulk, Brie. It's unbecoming in a college professor."

"Go away. I'm not sulking." She rolled over and looked out of the window. Just beyond the edge of the mountain, she could see the first traces of clouds. Was the weather changing?

"Give me some slack here, Brie. I'm not the bad guy."

She rolled back and sat up at that. "Neither am I, Jake, yet you hammer on me as if I were. I don't have the slightest idea who is doing this. Don't you think I've thought about it until I'm numb? If I had any suggestions, I'd tell you. I want it to stop. Nothing like this has happened to me before and I don't like it."

"I don't like it, either, and I'm only trying to figure out who's doing it."

"It's not my fault."

"I know that."

"You don't act like it sometimes," she muttered.

"Just put it down to my being a sore loser, okay? I'll try to modify my tactics."

"Take your interrogation *tactics* elsewhere. I'm not the suspect."

She frowned. What did he mean by sore loser? Just because he hadn't found the burglar yet didn't mean he'd lost.

He nodded, his eyes narrowed. "Yes, ma'am. Come on, we're going back to check out your car, then take it in for repair. It's supposed to rain and snow again, so you don't want it open to the elements."

"My insurance's going to go through the roof," she complained as they climbed into the jeep and began their journey back to Texarkana. "If they don't cancel me altogether."

"When we catch the guy, you can sue him to reimburse the insurance company. Relax, this kind of things happens and insurance companies know it."

"It doesn't happen to me. I've thought and thought until I'm blue in the face and can't imagine who would keep doing it or why."

Jake reached over and caught her eye. "We'll find him and stop him. Count on it!"

Mildly comforted, she settled back for the ride. It did no good to worry. She had faith in the legal system. Once they found the man, the break-ins would cease.

And so would her reason to be with Jake. So it didn't exactly make the future a win-win in her book.

Their time together would be so fleeting. She almost wished they'd never find the man, that he'd break in with great regularity, just so she could stay with Jake for protection.

It was late by the time they'd seen to Brianna's car. The clouds that had been peeping over the mountains obliterated the sun. The wind blew hard from the west, stirring up the snow, chilling the air. Brianna shivered as she climbed back into Jake's car.

"Want to eat here in town before we head back?" Jake asked when he joined her.

"Sure. Or we can go back to my place and fix spaghetti or something."

He hesitated. "We're having your house watched. I'd just as soon you not show up this weekend. If the offer is just as good at my apartment, we could eat there."

"Do you have more food at your apartment than you did at the cabin?" she asked suspiciously.

"No. But we're only a couple of minutes from the grocery store. We'll stop there first."

More playing house, she thought, walking beside Jake as he pushed the cart in the supermarket. She chose the ingredients she needed for a spaghetti dinner, remembering some of his tastes, learning a few new ones. Jake picked out a nice wine and before long they were through the checkout and on the way to his apartment.

While Brianna knew where Jake lived, she'd never visited. The apartment complex was one that was popular with singles with loads of amenities. She suspected he used the workout facility with regularity.

He led the way into the brick building, then down the ground floor hall to his door.

"The swinging singles lifestyle," she murmured after they left the elevator and he slipped his key into the lock.

"No, Mrs. Fenster lives two doors down. She's a widowed grandmother who's lived here for years. Nice lady, though." Opening the door, he stood aside so Brianna could enter.

"Good grief, it's as cold in here as outside." Shivering, Brianna looked around.

The room was almost as sterile as the cabin. The only signs that someone lived there were the stacks of books piled haphazardly on one table and a couple of old TV guides that lay on the floor beside a recliner. The rest of the decor could be considered early bachelor. A place to hang his hat, that's all this apartment was. Where was his home? Where did he keep his pictures and memorabilia from the past? His bedroom, maybe?

"Yeah, it's cold. Just a sec, and I'll turn on the heat. I shut it off thinking we'd be gone for several days." He led the way into the minuscule kitchen and dropped the bag on the counter.

"Why is it so cold? It feels like we're still outside."

"I leave the bathroom window open. I hate a stuffy place and this place always seems stuffy if I don't have some fresh air."

"Even in winter?"

"With the heat on, it's warm enough."

"Your bill must be huge. You're heating up half of Texarkana."

"It's worth it for fresh air. Come on, cooking dinner will warm you up."

"Oh, I get it now. This kitchen is much smaller than the one at the cabin so only one person at a time can work in it." She paused at the entry. It was a typical apartment galley kitchen, sink and counter on one side, stove and refrigerator opposite. And hardly room to swing a cat.

"Since you suggested dinner and are the better cook, I figured you could be that one person."

"It's your place. I really shouldn't intrude," she protested, half teasing.

He frowned with mock ferocity. "You don't want to eat my spaghetti. You'd be awake all night from heartburn."

Instead of being awake all night from heartache, she almost retorted.

Turning away from those knowing eyes, she began to unpack the grocery bag.

By the time dinner was ready, the apartment was warm. Jake had put on some soft music and drawn the drapes. They were cocooned in a world of their own.

They did not, however, linger over dinner. Jake mentioned that the weather report had predicted snow.

"And with the wind blowing the way it is, I don't want to be driving in a blizzard."

"We could stay in Texarkana if it's too bad to drive in," Brianna suggested.

"No, I wanted to spend the weekend at the cabin. We'll make it back tonight. I just don't want to be too late leaving."

She didn't have to go back with him. She could still call Sandy, or Josh for that matter.

Considering all her options, Brianna sipped the wine. Its warmth crept into every cell of her body. Raising her gaze to Jake, she knew she would return to his cabin with him. She was only pretending to herself that she would consider anything else.

The snowstorm hit before they reached the Oklahoma line. And, as Jake had feared, with the wind blowing so much, it felt like a blizzard trying to drive in it. The wind swirled the snow until visibility became almost nonexistent. The road was slick and treacherous. Even with the car in four-wheel drive, crawling along, they skidded more than once.

"Can you find the cabin in this?" Brianna asked at one point. She felt as if they had been driving blind since they left.

"Sure. We'll be there in another ten minutes or so," Jake answered easily.

"And then snowbound for how long?" she muttered.

"This looks bad, but it's because of the wind. Not that much is supposed to fall. But if it gets too deep for the car, we can always take the snowmobiles."

She hoped the storm would be of a short duration.

A weekend at Jake's cabin was all she was prepared for. She had to be back at work on Monday.

True to his word, they pulled up before the log cabin a few minutes later. Rushing from the car to the door, Jake held on to her hand. Since she could hardly see him standing beside her, she was glad for the support. She might have lost her way getting from the car to the cabin.

Once inside, with the raging storm shut firmly behind them, Brianna relaxed. She had been as tense in the car as if she'd been the one driving. But they were safe at home now.

Home. She looked around at the familiar room. She hadn't felt such a sense of homecoming in a long, long time.

"We made it," she said softly.

"Home safe." He leaned over and kissed her.

Six

Brianna closed the mathematics journal and gazed into the fire. She'd been reading all morning. Snow continued to fall steadily, though the wind had died during the night. So much for not a lot. They already had more than ten inches on the railing of the porch. The hushed air increased her sense of isolation.

Idly she wondered where Jake had gone. He'd been fussing around the place when she began to read after breakfast, then mumbled something about checking on the snowmobiles and left. How long ago had that been?

Caught up at last with her journals, she debated moving. She was warm and comfortable on the big sofa. The fire was dying, however, its feeble flames flickering as if they were gasping for fuel. She needed to replenish it to keep it going, but for the moment, she wanted to be lazy and not move.

There was so much that she needed to do. She had lesson plans to prepare. That had been the worst part about the break-ins, having her plans destroyed. She prided herself on being organized and ahead of the game.

She also had a paper she wanted to submit to one of

the mathematics journals, but needed to get her lesson plans finished before doing anything else.

Yet all she really wanted to do was find Jake and spend time with him.

Rubbing the ache in her breast, she remembered her determination to remain aloof, to refuse to give in to the emotions that flared whenever she came near the man.

Tough. She wanted Jake.

Rising, she tossed a couple of small logs on the fire, waiting until they caught before she replaced the screen and turned to the front window. Maybe she'd plan some suggestions on how he could fix up this place after all. It was a beautiful structure and the furniture was good, if a bit austere. He only needed a few accessories to turn it into a warm and welcoming home.

And if she succeeded, he'd think of her every time he used his cabin.

Smiling in satisfaction, she went in search of a notepad.

Brianna had a long list of things she wanted him to get by the time she stopped to prepare lunch. She heated some soup, and toasted the last of the French bread they'd bought in Texarkana. When everything was ready, she went to find Jake.

He was in the shed, tinkering with one of the snowmobiles. A portable heater gave some warmth, enough that he'd taken off his jacket and rolled up his sleeves. His hands were black with grease.

"What are you doing?" Brianna asked as she slid open the door just enough to enter, then closed it quickly behind her to keep out the snow and chill.

"This was running rough yesterday. Thought I'd take a look at it. You finished your reading?" He didn't look at her but continued adjusting a valve.

"Yes, both journals. And I made a list of things for you to buy. It's fun, actually, spending other people's money."

He looked up at that. "What?"

"For your cabin. I made a list of curtains, rugs, pillows, things like that. Then you need the rods and the pads and hooks and some bookcases. I noticed at your apartment how many books you had that are just stacked haphazardly. You really need some bookcases there, and here. That way you could have your books in both places—"

"You're running off at the mouth again. Are you upset?" His eyes narrowed as he studied her.

She shook her head. Not upset, just giddy being around him. Not that she could tell him that. God forbid that he should even guess.

"I fixed lunch. Soup and hot bread." She clamped down on the other words. She wouldn't babble!

"Be there in a sec." He increased the torque.

"Any time. I'll just simmer the soup and keep the bread in the oven. Though it could dry out." Turning abruptly, she headed back to the house.

Jake followed in only moments. While he washed at the sink, she served the meal.

"This is nice," he said as he sat down. "When I come up alone, I usually have sandwiches."

"It's too cold for sandwiches," she murmured, pleased he liked the modest lunch.

"I think the snow's letting up. We could go for a walk later if you wish," he suggested after the first pangs of hunger had been satisfied.

She nodded. "That'd get me out of the house. I don't think I can get cabin fever from one morning, but I wouldn't mind going for a walk."

She stared into the bowl of soup. Would her life ever get back to normal?

"I called into the station this morning. Nothing new," Jake said as if reading her mind.

She shrugged. "Is that good news? He hasn't broken into anything of mine now for a day."

"Two years ago you were involved pretty heavily with someone who obviously didn't return your feelings. What happened between you two beyond the obvious breakup? Was there anger, bitterness, any reason for retaliation?"

She blinked and met his gaze. Was this the policeman's way of distancing himself from personal involvement? Treat them both like third parties, take the personal out of the question?

"No reason for retaliation. No anger that I know of. Mostly bewilderment on my part," she replied slowly. "I mean when things ended, I didn't know what I'd done wrong."

"Surely there was some hurt, some regret, some feeling of wanting to change things, make them come right."

He spoke of his own feelings. Funny, until today he had thought he was coping. But the frustration of wanting this woman and not being able to have her threatened to swamp him. Two years ago, he'd made his decision, based on circumstances that appeared to have changed. Yet he didn't think he'd make a different decision.

Only—he still had regrets.

"So what if there is?" she asked defiantly. If he thought to excuse his behavior or offer some platitude—

"So maybe the man's trying a different tactic, one to make you aware of being alone, of needing him."

She stared at him in horror. Had Jake staged the break-ins just to be the hero riding in to save her? But there had been no need. A phone call and she would have been more than willing to see him again. She had longed for such a call.

No, that didn't make sense. Besides, he'd been with her when her car was broken into. And Jake was too honorable, too much a policeman to ever do anything criminal.

"I don't think I understand what you're talking about," she started. "I didn't walk out of the relationship. You…he did."

The phone rang. He leaned over and picked it up.

"Morgan." His eyes never left hers.

A tendril of fear snaked up her back. Was this a new report from the police about something else of hers damaged? Or had they found the man? Was the reason for her staying in Jake's cabin now gone?

"Thanks for the update. We'll be in and out, but keep me informed." He slid the receiver back in place.

"Another break-in?" she asked.

"No. Nothing to report. The information from your

neighbor wasn't enough to ID anyone. We know he's a man—too large to be a woman. We know his car's a dark SUV, so we're noting any that drive by your place."

Brianna shivered. "I hate this. I feel like I'm the prisoner and I didn't do anything wrong."

"I know it's a strain. Most police work is time-consuming. But we'll find him. He'll either make a mistake, or something will turn up to lead us to him. We'll get him."

"I just hope I'm not a basket case before then."

"You're doing fine, honey. There's nothing more I can do for you."

"You could hold me," she blurted out. Her eyes held his, the longing and uncertainty clearly written on her face.

He didn't move; his expression was hard, as if carved from granite.

"Forget it. I—it's just I feel so scared sometimes."

He made his feelings obvious. She felt like an idiot asking him to hold her.

"I don't think it's a good idea, Brie."

"Yeah, you're right. I'm a big girl now. I don't need someone to hold me and kiss things better."

Jake closed his eyes momentarily, snapped them open. "It's all right to be afraid. We're going to protect you. We'll find him, I promise."

She nodded, fiddling with the last of her bread. How could she have asked him to hold her? Good grief, she wasn't some baby that needed coddling. She was a mature...

Tears welled in her eyes. She was scared, damn it.

Her entire life had been disrupted and she didn't even know why. She just wanted him to hold her.

"Come on, baby." He reached over and lifted her from the chair, leading her into the living room. Sinking down on the sofa, Jake pulled her into his lap and put his arms around her. "This isn't a good idea because of all the lascivious thoughts that race through my mind when you're in my arms," he whispered in her ear.

In contrast to his words, his touch was devoid of passion. His arms held her against his solid chest; his chin rested against her hair. He gently rubbed her back.

Brianna sighed, snuggled closer and relaxed for the first time in days. She closed her eyes and gave herself up to the enjoyment of being held. Jake made everything seem safe. He would find the bad guy and lock him up. She believed him. Things would go back to normal and she'd be safe.

Alone, facing the future without the man she loved, but she'd be safe. Thanks to him.

Jake reviewed all his transgressions, trying to see which had been so heinous to warrant this kind of torture. Holding Brianna, just to offer comfort, was hell. He wanted to kiss her, make love to her. Find a spot for her in his world, despite all the odds against them, and keep her for himself.

It wouldn't work. Josh made sure he knew that. She must know it, too. She never spoke about the time when they were dating.

Brianna found herself memorizing every second. She drew a deep breath, savoring Jake's special scent. She buried her nose in his chest and held her breath to better remember each different aroma. The smell of his soap, of his after-shave, the laundry detergent used on his shirt, and his own masculine scent that opened the gates to wild, exciting dreams.

She listened to his heartbeat, slow and steady as it pumped the life's blood of the man who was so precious to her.

She felt his arms across her back, the hard steel of his thighs beneath her own, the strength of his chest as he cradled her, offering comfort and support. Could she freeze a moment in time? Could she end everything and stay suspended in this minute? She wished it could be. If she lived to be a hundred, she would never forget Jake Morgan. She knew she'd love him all her life.

She also knew life was unfair. She'd lost her parents when she was a little girl. She'd missed many things young girls shared with their mothers. And just loving a man didn't mean he'd love in return. Sighing softly, she felt the tears again, but this time they were for what might have been and was not.

"I'm probably crushing you," she whispered, tightening her arms around his neck and bringing her face up to meet his gaze. His lips were mere inches away. She felt his breath fan her cheeks, felt the heat radiating from his body.

"No."

Her smile wobbled. When he cupped her face with his hands and brushed the teardrops from her spiky lashes, her heart melted. He looked worried about her.

"I'll keep you safe, Brie. I won't let him hurt you."

"I'm all right. It's just—I know. I won't worry

anymore."

"Oh, I don't know. Maybe you should start worrying—about me." With that, Jake brought his mouth down on hers in a mind-blowing kiss.

Had this really been what she sought? Not comfort, but bliss? When she was in his arms, she didn't worry or think about the future or regret the past. She only felt. Felt the wonder of his touch, the magic of his embrace, the shimmering sensations that sizzled through her.

The world spun dizzyingly as he laid her down on the sofa and pressed her into the cushions. Endless moments of spiraling delight whirled around and around as their kiss went on and on. Breathing was forgotten. The blood rushed through her veins, heating every cell, pounding in her ears. Time ceased. Earthly cares hung suspended as they were lost in a world of their own making, one of wonder and passion and love.

When Jake pulled back at last, it was too soon. Brianna gave a small moan of protest, and he kissed her again, then sat up.

"We're moving beyond comfort. Come on, let's take that walk." He rose and went to the window. "It's stopped snowing. It's still overcast, but we won't get wet walking."

Brianna stared at his back in startled surprise. What happened? One moment he was kissing her like there was no tomorrow, the next calmly suggesting they take a walk!

Feeling totally confused, she sat up and pulled back her hair. There was something wrong when she couldn't keep his attention in the throes of passion. Sighing, she rose on shaky legs and headed for the bedroom.

"I'll be out in a minute," she said as she closed the door behind her. Leaning against it for a long moment, she closed her eyes, reliving the kiss. The kiss of a lifetime—and he wanted to go for a walk in the snow. She shook her head and pushed away from the door. She brushed her hair and quickly braided it to keep it from blowing.

Her eyes sparkled back at her in the mirror, her cheeks were bright with color and her lips were rosy. She turned away, her heart heavy.

Jake stood by the door already wearing his shearling jacket. Brianna quickly donned her own jacket and pulled on a knit cap and woolen mittens.

"I'm ready," she said brightly. She'd go home tomorrow, no matter what.

Stepping out onto the porch, Brianna caught her breath. The air was so cold it almost snapped. Snow blanketed everything, from the tree limbs bent beneath the weight, to the distinctive shape of Jake's car. Smiling in delight at the pristine setting, she boldly stamped down the stairs, making the first marks in the white expanse.

"This is great! We're the first to walk in it."

"Yeah, want to help shovel?" He stood on the porch, watching her, then scanning the area from habit.

"No. And you're not shoveling anything now, either. Come on, you said walk, let's walk."

Bravely Brianna set off, hoping she didn't wind up in some drift. The snow covered her ankles, puffing away from each step as she forged into virgin territory. Two seconds later, Jake joined her, his longer stride eating up the distance.

"Doesn't this remind you of being a kid? We couldn't wait to be finished with chores when it snowed so we could play," she reminisced happily. Tilting her head back to look up at him, she waited for his memories. Were they as happy as hers?

He shook his head. "You forget, I'm from Denver. We didn't have expanses of open land like this. I lived in apartments that had parking lots plowed as soon as the first flake fell."

Brianna exhaled, watching the cloud hang suspended in front of her before it gradually dissipated. She eyed the trees ahead of them, then smiled. "So you didn't partake in snowball fights?" she asked innocently.

"Sure, just not often. There weren't a lot of kids around where I lived. Why, you want to fight?"

She shook her head. "Not really. We could make a snowman."

"What about snow angels? I want to see an award-winning angel."

Without any warning, she turned and fell back into the soft snow. Slowly she raised her arms up and down, packing the snow beneath her. She opened and closed her legs.

"For a perfect snow angel, I need help to get up. Otherwise I'll mess up the outline," she said, carefully drawing her arms away from the snow and holding out her hands. "Don't step on my skirt!" she warned.

Jake laughed as he reached over and clasped her hands, pulling her upright. Together they studied the outline in the snow.

"Perfect or what?" she asked triumphantly, her heart racing with exhilaration.

She enjoyed seeing him laugh. Could she get him to do it again?

"Perfect." Only his eyes were on her, not the outline in the snow.

Brianna was mesmerized by the lights in his dark gaze. "It's all in the technique. And not getting up by yourself. My brothers were too impatient to wait for anyone to help them up. So their angels…"

She didn't care what her brothers had done; neither did Jake. She wanted him to kiss her again. Like he had on the sofa. More than comfort, much more.

She almost cried out in protest when he stepped away and continued walking. "I'll remember. It's the technique."

"Like building a snowman," she said, hurrying to catch up.

"That's got a technique to it, as well?" he asked.

"Sure. Josh always wanted to build the biggest one in the world. So we'd roll the bottom forever, until it was huge. Then the next ball would get too big for us to lift. You have to practice some moderation."

"That was when you were kids. How big do you think we could make one now?"

"Oh, no, not another I-want-to-build-the-biggest-snowman-in-the-world person," she wailed.

"We can at least make one bigger than your brother ever did."

Giving in to the fun, Brianna kept up a running

commentary as they rolled the balls to make the snowman. She told Jake about escapades as a child. How her mother worked hard to keep the three children occupied during the long winter days. Chores, activities, quiet time, all came bubbling out in happy reminiscences.

Jake listened, fascinated. He had little to offer in return, but it didn't seem to matter. Brianna had enough stories to keep them entertained all day and night if she chose to keep going.

When it came time to lift the second ball, they worked together, staggering beneath its weight, carefully setting it on the base, packing snow around it to keep it from rolling off. Then the head. Jake lifted it by himself.

"We need a picture," Brianna said when they put the finishing touches on the face. The snowman was as tall as she was. "Josh will never believe this without a picture. Did you bring your phone?"

"Of course. Stand beside him and we'll have something to compare it to."

He snapped several photographs, capturing the delight in her expression, the rosy cheeks, the radiant blue of her eyes. He'd give her some, but one or two he wouldn't share. They'd be for him alone.

"This will show Josh," she said with glee, looking at the pictures a minute later. "He has a tendency to believe he knows everything, from what's best for me to how Jase should expand the ranch. Let him deny this!" She gave a fist pump, her eyes dancing. "This is the greatest snowman ever."

Jake was curiously silent. His gaze firmly on the snowman, he only nodded absently to Brianna's comments, lost in thought.

"Earth to Jake." She shook his arm.

"What?"

"Where were you?"

"Just thinking. Ready to head back?"

"Almost. Let's walk just a little farther."

He missed the gleam in her eye. She kept her face turned a bit lest he guess her plans. Gleeful anticipation rose. She felt like a kid again, carefree and happy.

They walked beyond their prized snowman, the walking growing more difficult as the snow grew deeper. Soon they were into the trees that lined the open space around Jake's cabin. Brianna paused, leaning over to scrape snow off her boot. Jake continued walking slowly so she could catch up.

Grabbing a handful of snow, Brianna packed it, then tossed it up and caught it. Tossed again, caught it.

Jake turned, eyeing the snowball suspiciously. "We're not having a snowball fight," he stated.

"Stuffy," she replied.

"You'd lose big time, sweetheart."

Warily he watched the ball as she tossed it up and caught it again.

"Wanna bet?" she asked softly, stepping closer. Jake took a step back. Brianna advanced another foot. He moved back an equal distance.

Grinning in triumph, she let it fly. The snowball hit the heavily laden branch above him and a cloud of snow rained down on Jake, covering him from head to foot.

Laughing aloud, Brianna turned and ran for her life. She'd done this so many times with Jase and Josh she knew the routine. If she could only make the cabin, she'd be—

He tackled her from behind, forcing her face down in the snow. She was laughing too hard to resist. Turning her face to breathe, she couldn't control the giggles. He'd looked stunned as the snow began to slide off the branch.

Rolling her onto her back, he snatched off her hat and grabbed a handful of snow, packing it in around her neck.

"Nooo! That's cold. Stop! Stop!" she shrieked. She tried to escape, but he lay across her legs and held her firmly.

"Damn straight it's cold. Just like the snow down my neck." He reached for another handful of snow but she batted it away, showering them both with the icy powder.

"Okay, I give up. I'm sorry." Her giggles belied the sincerity of her apology.

"Not good enough." He scooped up another handful, threatening.

Brianna knocked it away and reached up to pull him down. Her lips were cold, his cheek colder. She kissed him gently. "I'll gladly grovel, but before the fire, please?"

He captured her cheeks in his cold hands and gazed down at her, his eyes dark and mysterious. She looked lovely. Her face was bright with color, her eyes sparkling, her lips curved in the most delectable smile.

"You're driving me crazy, do you know that?"

"I'm just trying to have some fun," she said, her smile warm and loving.

Jake rested his forehead against hers, closing his eyes as they lay on the cold ground. Taking a deep breath, he stood, then reached down to pull her upright.

"Cold?" he asked, watching her as she tried to get the snow out of her neckline.

"Just where I'm covered in snow."

She couldn't keep from laughing, though. This had been the most fun she'd had in years.

"Me, too. Let's head back. This time, you stay right with me the whole way."

"As close as you'll let me," she murmured, falling into step as he turned toward home.

Jake was careful to keep a couple of feet between them. She didn't know why, but suspected it was to keep his hands to himself. She wished he'd reach out to her. She'd take her mittens off in a second if he'd show any sign of wanting to hold her hand. Instead, he seemed more aloof, more distant than ever. As if they were really the strangers they had become over the past two years. As if the time they'd spent together these past few days meant nothing. Was she only a case to be solved? Was it only some sense of duty that kept him near?

Jake built up the fire, told Brianna to change into dry clothes, then left to work on the snowmobile. Brianna watched him walk away, a feeling of déjà vu sweeping over her. He'd walked away before, and she hadn't known then that it was goodbye. He was pulling away from her again. They'd enjoyed the afternoon until she'd clearly shown she wanted another kiss. If he'd slammed a door in her face, he couldn't have been any clearer.

"So what is the big deal? You've kissed me before,"

she said to the empty room. Getting no answer, she headed for the bedroom to change into dry clothes.

Dinner proved to be a strained affair. Neither spoke except to request food to be passed. When Jake said he'd do the dishes, Brianna acquiesced with speed, taking it as a certain indication he didn't want her around.

"I need to get back tomorrow," she said as she carried her plate to the sink.

"No need, you can stay here—"

"It's not a question of my staying here. I have a life to get back to. I appreciate your having me this weekend. And I hope there's been enough time to catch whoever is doing the break-ins. But I have things I need to do. I do have a life apart from being the victim of a crime, you know."

"Hot date to get back to?" he asked sardonically.

"Maybe," she returned, anxious to end this. She longed for her own place.

"Thought you weren't involved with anyone right now." His eyes focused on her as if he could see inside her soul.

She turned and stared him straight in the eye. "That's really not your concern anymore, is it? We dated a couple of years ago, then stopped. Since then, my life, private and public, is my own. It has nothing to do with you."

He clenched his jaw at her attack, his features still. Only the glittering heat in his eyes gave away his strong feelings.

"You're correct. Your life is no concern of mine. I'll drive you back in the morning. I don't want to chance the roads tonight."

"Tomorrow is fine. Thank you." Head held high, she walked into the bedroom and closed the door with exaggerated care. Methodically she prepared for bed, her mind spinning. She had wanted him to say something, anything, to indicate he cared about her. Nothing. She meant nothing. It was past time for her to get on with her life. And Jake would not be a part of it.

Seven

"The bathroom is yours," Brianna said as she came into the kitchen the next morning. She refused to look at Jake, though she could see he wore a shirt this morning. She'd packed her bag and set it by the front door. Her jacket and hat were on top. She was ready to leave as soon as they finished eating.

Operating on autopilot, she refused to dwell on anything. She had her whole future to think. Today she just wanted to get home.

She went through the motions of cooking oatmeal, setting the table and pouring the coffee as if in a trance. She only had a little longer, then she'd be free. Free of the need to watch every word, every gesture, lest she give herself away. Free of the constant hunger to touch him, listen to him, look at him. Free of the heartache that threatened to drown her.

Hearing the shower, she paused for a moment as she realized sadly their time of playing house was coming to an end. However brief, for the most part it had been interesting. She drew out the list of items she'd made and set it at his place. Whether he implemented her ideas or not, she no longer cared. She wouldn't be coming back to the cabin.

They were silent as Jake drove back to Texarkana. The highway had been cleared and they made good time. He pulled up before her house and turned off the engine.

"Let me go in first to check things out to make sure the place is secure," he said, opening his door.

She nodded, then alighted. Reaching for her bag, she gave him her key. Her chin held high, she led the way up the snowy walk. She'd have to shovel it later. It would give her something to do.

Opening the door, Jake walked in while Brianna stood to one side, waiting. His sweep was brief. He returned and paused beside her. "No sign of any unlawful entry," he said formally.

"Thank you, Officer. I appreciate your help." She stepped inside and pushed the door shut. He caught it before it closed all the way and held it a moment.

"I'll pick you up in the morning and take you to the college. When your car's ready, I'll give you a ride to pick it up."

"That's not necessary, but thank you. I have friends—"

"I'll pick you up in the morning." His hard tone brooked no refusal.

She swallowed. "Very well." Pushing on the door this time shut it. She stood for a long moment, listening as he started his car and drove away.

Fortunately, she had plenty to do. It kept thought at bay. She worked on lesson plans, shoveled the walk and visited briefly with her neighbors. Life had returned to normal.

The next morning, Brianna stood at her front window, watching the street. She and Jake hadn't set a time when he would come, yet she knew he'd be there early enough for her first class. He was too good a police officer to have let something like her class schedule slip past an investigation.

She wondered what else he'd uncovered in trying to solve this case. He couldn't know she didn't date since he kept trying to find out who she was seeing. Why? Did he really suspect a love affair gone bad might be behind these break-ins as retaliation or was he simply curious?

When his car pulled to a stop in front of her house, she put on her coat, gathering her briefcase, she let herself out of the house. He opened the passenger door for her.

"Good morning."

"Good morning." She could be as formal as he. The drive to the university took less than five minutes. He circled the wide circle that was the center of the campus and came to a halt before the Thompson Building. She glanced at him before opening the door, not meeting his eyes, her gaze on his chin. "Thank you for the ride."

"Your car will be ready at two. I'll pick you up and take you over."

"I can—"

"Don't argue, Brie. Just do as you're told."

"Let me tell you, Jake Morgan, I do as I please, not as some bossy cop tells me."

He ran his fingers through his hair and glared at her. "I didn't sleep worth a damn last night. I've a million things to do. If I take time to come pick you up to take you to get your car, you had better be waiting right here!" He leaned over her, almost shouting in his frustration.

"And there's no reason for you to do that. I have friends who can take me. I don't need to add to your million things to do!"

He took a calming breath and clenched his jaw. She could see the tightness.

"Never mind. Thank you. I'll be waiting right here at two."

She hopped out of the car and slammed the door. Waiting as he accelerated away, she turned and headed for her office. Why hadn't he slept last night? And if he were so inconvenienced at having to chauffeur her somewhere, why not let someone else do it? She had friends who would be glad to give her a lift. She needn't rely on him.

Shaking her head, she started up the steps. Since her office was on the third floor, she liked taking the stairs as a form of exercise. They flanked the ends of the U-shaped building. The windows at each landing were open in the stairwell, which did nothing to keep the wind out. Each floor had a heavy door that handled that task.

Running up the first flight, Brianna was so busy thinking about Jake she didn't at first see the other person in the stairwell. Suddenly he was in front of her, pushing against her, yanking her briefcase. She staggered, scraped her head against the concrete wall, lost her balance, then fell down the stairs, bumping every one as she tried her best to stop her fall.

She came to rest in a heap at the landing. Her wrist hurt, her head burned and her ankle throbbed. Gingerly she sat up. Wincing as she pulled some muscles, she reached up and found blood on her forehead.

She couldn't hear a thing. No footsteps, no one appeared to still be in the stairwell.

Someone had pushed her! And stolen her briefcase!

Trying to stand, she groaned and sank back to the floor. Her ankle hurt too much to bear any weight.

Hearing some voices outside, she called for help. Thankfully two students arrived in seconds.

Brianna sat alone in the cubicle at the county hospital's emergency room, her legs dangling over the edge of the examination table, when she heard Jake's voice. The scrape on her head had been cleaned, treated and covered with a bandage. Her wrist and ankle, both sprained, had been x-rayed. Her foot was in a walking cast and her arm was wrapped in an Ace bandage.

She'd answered all the questions the campus police had asked and now awaited someone from that department to take her home. Her department head had been notified and arranged to cover her classes if she wasn't able to be there when they started again.

She counted the seconds from the time she first heard his voice until he found her. Eight. Pretty good. But then, she'd known he was good.

"What the hell happened?"

Jake burst into the cubicle like a bull in a raging

temper. The waves of frustration and anger radiated from him like steam from a hot spring. His badge was clipped to his coat, his hair wind-tossed and his eyes narrowed and lethal. She shivered, glad she wasn't the focal point of that dangerous look.

"Someone wanted my briefcase, I guess," she said. "Maybe that's what they wanted all along. Maybe the break-ins will stop now."

"Are you all right?" His voice tempered. He leaned over her, his fingers gently brushing near the bandage on her forehead. Gently he pushed her hair behind her ear. Some of it was still matted with blood, though the nurse had tried her best to clean it when cleaning the scrape.

"I will be fine." She swallowed hard, blinking to keep tears away. She longed to reach out for comfort, to have him hold her and keep her safe. Taking a shaky breath, she tried to smile.

"Hell, Brie, I said I'd keep you safe and look what happened." The anger was leashed, his voice soft and gentle.

"It's hardly your fault," she said, reaching out to touch his shoulder, the tactile feel of his coat anchoring her. Who was offering comfort to whom? she wondered.

"I should have walked you to your office," he muttered.

"Oh, come on, Jake, be reasonable. Are you going to shadow me all the livelong day? You delivered me to my office building. No one could predict he'd try something like this. Every other incident has been against my property. He did bump me, but if I hadn't lost my balance, I might not have fallen. It happened so fast, I couldn't react. By the time I realized what was happening, I was already at the bottom of the steps."

He looked over her, touched her wrist lightly. "Anything broken?"

She shook her head, then winced as it throbbed. "No, just a few scrapes and bruises. And a sprained wrist and ankle. I'll be fine in a few weeks. Really."

"What was in your briefcase?" The switch from concerned friend to official cop was instant.

"Nothing important. Lesson plans. God, I can't believe I have to do some of them over again. This is getting ridiculous."

"There had to be more than lesson plans. Think."

The curtain to the cubicle slid open and a young resident entered. "Is this your ride home, Professor?" he asked, eyeing Jake suspiciously.

Brianna looked at Jake, her eyebrows raised questioningly.

"Yes, I'm taking her home. Any instructions?" Jake asked.

"We went through them a few minutes ago. She should stay off that foot for the next couple of days. Then she can walk on it as she feels comfortable, providing she wears the support. We've already scheduled a follow-up appointment."

A nurse arrived pushing a wheelchair. Before anyone could move, Jake lifted Brianna and placed her in the chair. "I'll take care of her and see she follows your orders," he said gruffly.

Who says? she wanted to ask, but prudently kept quiet. There would be time to deal with a bossy Jake after they left the hospital.

The nurse assisted her into the car, and collapsed the wheel chair and let him put it in the back of the jeep.

"It's on loan. Since you can't use crutches because of your wrist, and the doctor's adamant you keep off that foot, I arranged to borrow the wheel chair."

"I have two steps up into my house," she commented, feeling a bit groggy and still disoriented.

"We'll manage." He drove her home, took her keys and opened her door, then returned to the car and lifted her out.

"I can use the chair they gave me, hop up the two steps. Put me down. I weigh too much."

"You're not heavy. I think you've lost weight over the past couple of years. You should eat more."

"I eat plenty. Put me down." Her arm encircled his neck and even through the bulky clothing, she could feel the strength of his chest and arms. She longed to rest her head against his shoulder, longed to give up and let him take care of her, if only for today.

"I'll put you down when we get inside." He walked through the house and directly into the bedroom. Depositing her gently on the bed, he helped her remove her coat and remaining shoe. Drawing a knitted afghan over her, he stood and looked around.

He'd seen the room before, of course, when checking out her place. But now he thought about it being her bedroom. A glance at the big bed and he instantly wondered when she had acquired it and why.

A single woman living alone didn't really need a queen-size bed. But that was the thing—had she always been alone?

Not liking the trend of his thoughts, he looked at Brianna. She was watching him, a puzzled expression on her face.

"I have to check in at the station, then go home and get a few things. I'll be back in a couple of hours," he said. "I'll stop at your neighbors and see if she can sit with you. Do you need anything before I go?"

"You're coming back? What for? Martha will be glad to help me. She won't mind."

"I'm staying here until you're mobile."

"No!"

"Don't argue."

"Jake, you can't stay here. I don't have another bedroom." Her mind was scrambled. There had to be other reasons why he couldn't stay.

"I'll sleep in the living room."

"That sofa is hardly big enough for someone your size."

"I'll manage. Rest until I get back. I bet those pain pills the doctor gave you are kicking in about now."

She did feel like she was floating, but still had to make herself clear.

"I don't need you to come back. I have neighbors—"

"I've already taken the time off. Might as well stay here as at the cabin. If we'd stayed there, this wouldn't have happened."

"I do have a job," she said.

"What was in your briefcase?" he asked again.

"You keep asking that."

"I'm trying to find a reason that makes sense for all this."

The only reason he was back in her life was because of the recent events. Once he solved the case, would she ever see him again?

"So far nothing has made any sense. I had my attendance book for all my fall classes. My calendar for the spring semester." She paused in thought. "An outline of a journal article I'm doing. An invitation to a faculty tea honoring a new professor in the computer science department." She closed her eyes, trying to remember everything that had been in her briefcase. She was so concerned about the lost lesson plans that she had difficulty remembering the other items. "Let me think...the mail I picked up last Thursday from my box but hadn't read. You wouldn't let me take work with me to the cabin, remember? And I didn't get to it yesterday. And then my lesson plans—or the start of them anyway."

He frowned, frustrated. "Why would anyone want any of it? Is the article about some breakthrough?"

"Not really, just a different adaptation on an already much-discussed theorem. It'll get me some brownie points with the higher-ups, but it's certainly not worth stealing. Besides, if anyone used it, we'd know instantly who the culprit was."

"The campus police said you didn't recognize the assailant."

"No, he was tall, taller than I am anyway. He wore a ski mask, a dark blue jacket and dark jeans. It all happened so fast, I didn't notice anything more."

"You're a bright woman. You must have something someone wants—or wanted if he got what he was after today. Think about it while I'm gone."

"I don't need you to stay here, Jake," she said once again. She felt like a baby and didn't want him taking care of her.

He leaned over and brushed back her hair, cupping her chin with his warm palm. "I need to stay. I need to make sure you're all right." He brushed his lips across her forehead. The touch so light, Brianna wondered if she imagined it.

She lay back against the pillows and tried to relax. She was keyed up from both the attack and the thought of Jake staying with her for a day or so. Her mind, however, was growing fuzzy as the pain meds took hold.

She'd enjoyed having one place in life where she didn't have memories of Jake. Now that would all change if he moved in, took over and imprinted himself on every inch of her home.

Sighing in defeat, she closed her eyes. They were linked. Inexorably linked. She couldn't fight fate. She could only go along for the ride, however long it lasted this time.

Brianna dozed off and on all day, aware of Martha fussing over her a bit. That Jake had returned. Conscious that someone else was moving around her place but too lethargic to do anything she rolled over and drifted back to sleep.

When she awoke in the late afternoon, she was wide-awake and hungry. Gingerly she sat up, shifting to the edge of the bed until her feet reached the floor. Her ankle throbbed. She considered the distance to the bathroom and hesitated.

Jake appeared in the doorway. "Need help?" he asked, lounging casually against the jamb.

She glanced up, struck again by how tough and dangerous he looked leaning there watching her. In the dim light of the room, he was cloaked in shadows.

"I guess I do. My ankle hurts and I don't think I'm ready to walk on it."

He straightened and walked toward her. "Which is what the doctor said. No walking on it for a couple of days." Without any apparent effort, he scooped her up and headed to the bathroom. He deposited her inside and stepped out. "Call when you're finished," he said just before the door clicked shut.

He had the wheel chair at the door when she was ready to leave the bathroom. Hopping jarred her head and ankle too much to try that.

Jake had prepared dinner. He mentioned it was ready as he pushed her into the living room and through to the small dining alcove. She'd taken time while in the bathroom to brush her hair and wash what she could of her face with her one good hand.

Soft music played from her stereo, the curtains had been drawn against the growing twilight and the lamps gave a warm glow to the room. She wished again she had a fireplace. The evenings they'd spent before his at the cabin had been wonderful.

Most of the time she spent with Jake was wonderful. "Dinner."

Her small dining table was big enough for two.

Which suited her. She rarely had anyone over for a meal. She'd rather meet friends at a restaurant where there was room for all.

"This is delicious," Brianna said a few moments later when she tasted his chicken casserole.

"Thanks. It's easy."

"Somehow I didn't picture you cooking," she murmured. Plenty of men cooked. Her brothers were excellent cooks, though neither particularly liked to. But she hadn't pictured Jake cooking.

"I have to eat. Do you think I eat out every meal?" he replied, sitting opposite her with his own plate.

She shrugged. "Or ate donuts," she teased.

They'd eaten out a lot when dating. She'd cooked for him at her apartment a couple of times. And, of course, she'd cooked the meals at the cabin.

"Where did you learn to cook?" she asked.

"At home. When I was a kid, my uncle didn't get home until late, so I usually started dinner. Cooked the entire meal most nights."

"You lived with your uncle, I remember," She'd known he was an only child. When she had asked him about his parents once long ago, he'd merely mentioned they were dead. Then quickly changed the subject.

"From the time I was six until I went to college."

"Just the two of you?" she asked.

"Yes. He never married."

She looked at him, wondering about a lot of things. He never talked about his past. It hadn't seemed that important two years ago. They'd been caught up in the present and they'd only dated a few months.

Only long enough for her to fall in love.

What had his childhood been like? He hadn't told her about it. She'd sure talked enough about growing up on the ranch.

"Tell me about your uncle," she said, determined to change that.

He looked at her and shrugged. "What's to tell? He was a cop. We shared an apartment. I learned to cook."

"Do you see much of him now?"

He shook his head. "He died when I was in college."

"Longevity does not seem to run in your family," she commented.

He smiled wryly. "They were all accidents. My folks were killed in an airplane crash. My uncle was a cop, but he didn't die on duty. He was killed when he fell from a tall ladder, trying to help a friend put up storm windows. Hit his head on the curb and died on the spot."

"Was he the reason you became a cop?"

"Yeah."

"So you don't have any family living?"

He shook his head once, his eyes narrowed as if he was trying to guess what she was leading up to.

"I lost my parents, but I always had Jase and Josh. Now I have Shannon, too. I wished we lived closer. I always wanted a sister when I was growing up."

"Jase's wife?" he clarified.

She nodded, smiling and looking over into the living room where she had their photograph on a shelf.

"That's their wedding picture, on the second shelf. Isn't she cute? You'd think Jase invented love the way he's so crazy about her," she said wistfully.

She envied her older brother the love he'd found. He and his wife didn't mind everyone in the world knowing how much they adored each other. She wished she had the same kind of love.

"So your grand love affair didn't pan out," he said softly.

She blinked, hurt he'd mock her. He didn't need to rub her nose in the fact he didn't love her. And he needn't be cruel about it, either. With dignity, she raised her chin.

"I guess not. I'm not ashamed of feeling the way I do."

"I'm sorry, Brie."

She knew he meant it. He wasn't a cruel man, merely one who didn't love her.

She nodded, toying with the last bit on her plate. Restlessly, she shoved it aside.

"Thank you for dinner. It was delicious."

"Coffee?" Jake rose and gathered the plates, heading for the kitchen.

"Yes. There's some brandy over the refrigerator. I want some of that, too."

A timeless remedy for aches and pains of all kinds.

She struggled to maneuver the wheel chair with one hand, going in a semicircle.

"Here," he said, coming up behind her and deftly propelling her into the living room next to the sofa. Two swift moves and she was sitting on the sofa with a jar that set her head to pounding.

A minute later, Jake brought their mugs filled with fragrant coffee and the hint of brandy. Handing her one, he sat beside her on the sofa, resting his arm across the back, his fingers touching her hair.

"Not too much liquor, you still have medication in your system," he said when she sipped the hot beverage.

"Still tastes good," she said, taking a deep breath of the aroma.

"If I could change things for you, I would," he said in a low voice, dropping his hand to her shoulder, pulling her closer until she lay snuggled against his side.

"Wishing it won't make it so," she replied sadly.

"No, you can't make people love you no matter how much you might want them to." He'd learned that himself the hard way.

Brianna took a gulp of hot coffee. It burned all the way down, which jolted her out of the maudlin mood she was fast sinking into.

"So, did anything turn up today while I slept?" she asked, determined to keep the regrets at bay, at least until she was alone in her room.

"Nothing about the perpetrator. No one saw him but you. However, your briefcase turned up in a trash can behind the geology building. Empty."

"At least that wasn't lost. It was a gift to me from my brothers when I got my Ph.D. I'll be glad to have it back."

"We've pretty much eliminated the Air Force angle. Most of the people we've talked to didn't even know you worked for them."

"Honestly, are you telling everyone I know?" she asked. "I think I'm supposed to be circumspect about the job."

"We're questioning people who might have some leads for us."

"The work at the Air Force is a supposed secret. I didn't tell people because I didn't want anyone pestering me to reveal anything I shouldn't."

"Most of the people we've interviewed were impressed. They aren't going to try to pick your brain."

"So you don't think it's related to that work. But how can it be connected to the college?"

"Beats me, unless you have some top-secret formula for fattening cattle that some ranching syndicate's trying to get."

She chuckled. "No. I leave that to Josh and Jase. I go home to help out sometimes, but I'm not passionately in love with ranching like those two. Ever been on a cattle ranch?"

"Nope. I like thinking that beef comes in neat little packages in the supermarket, rather than covered in hide and mooing."

"A realist, I see."

Even if he knew nothing about cattle and horses, she'd bet he'd fit right in. There was something about men like him and her brothers and the ranch hands on Rafter C that spoke of confidence and assurance. They knew who they were, what they were capable of. Even the arrogance was similar. She smiled, wondering how he'd like meeting one or both of her brothers.

Taking a sip of her coffee, she savored the warmth. It had cooled enough to be consumed without burning. The dollop of brandy slid down smoothly. Soon the ache in her ankle and wrist would fade. Maybe even the ache in her heart.

"I see what you mean about no fireplace. Wish we were back at the cabin," Jake murmured, shifting a bit lower on the sofa, resting his legs beside hers on the coffee table. He settled Brianna into a more comfortable position, so she was leaning half on him, half against the sofa.

"Are you going to buy the things I suggested?" she asked, curious.

"Sure, if you go with me. Your list still doesn't tell me exactly what to buy."

"I was very clear." He was on his own for shopping. The time for playing house had ended.

"Then what did you mean by pictures?" he asked.

"Pictures, you know, images captured and framed to be put on a wall."

He glanced around her room, noting the soft Monet reproductions, the photographs that were displayed on shelves. Then he looked down at her.

"You choose," he said softly. "Something that will remind me of this place. It's nice, relaxing, pretty. Like you." Lowering his head, he kissed her. He tasted of coffee and brandy and male heat.

Brianna moved against his, savoring every second.

He took the cup from her numb fingers and placed it beside his on the table. Turning her, he dragged her across his chest, kissing her again and again, his hands threading through her silky hair, rubbing the length of her spine.

Her breath caught, her heart pounded. She snuggled closer, wanting to become a part of him, wanting nothing to separate them ever. Her hands clutched his broad shoulders, the sting in her wrist unnoticed because of the overwhelming sensations that shimmered through her.

He kissed her over and over, as if she were life-giving water and he a dying man in the desert. His hands caressed and petted. She was burning up with longings and burgeoning desire. Her senses were intoxicated and all reality was suspended as she floated on a cloud of sheer emotion.

She wanted more. She would have willingly given anything he asked. But all he wanted were kisses. Mind-drugging kisses. Kisses that brought a greater high than anything else she'd ever known.

Dang it, why couldn't he love her? She was so crazy about him she thought she'd go crazy, and he was sorry he couldn't love her.

But he could kiss her enough that she knew nothing else would ever satisfy her again. Kiss her enough that she knew she'd long for similar embraces all her life. Nothing would ever measure up.

And it wasn't fair. If he didn't want her, he should not be spoiling her for every other man in the world. She would never be satisfied with anyone else. She wanted Jake Morgan.

Eight

The phone rang, waking Brianna. She took a moment to realize she was still in bed. Her headache was gone. Her ankle throbbed. Her wrist ached. She stretched out to reach the phone. "Hello?"

"How are you feeling this morning?" Jake's familiar voice came through loud and clear.

She blinked and slowly sat up, bunching the pillow against the headboard. The sun was shining brightly.

"What time is it?" she asked, still feeling groggy.

"It's after ten. I thought you'd be up by now. Did I wake you?"

"Yes, but it's okay. It's too late to sleep. Where are you?" She refused to think about last night. Her fingers pressed against her lips. They were slightly swollen. Despite her best intentions, she remembered every single kiss.

"Your neighbors are staying with you until I get home. I'm at the station. I'm going by the college in a little while to get a list of all your students from the last two years. Then you and I are going over them one by one to see who might have any kind of grudge—real or imagined—to plague you like this."

"That's going to be a lot of students, I teach several classes."

"If there's something there, you're bound to recognize it. See you later."

Martha must have heard her on the phone because just then there was a soft knock on her door.

The neighbor kindly helped Brianna bathe and dress. Her husband was in the living room, standing guard if needed.

Brianna was touched at her neighbors' willingness to step in. She really thought the break ins had stopped. The robber had checked out everything she owned.

Maybe tomorrow she could return to work. There was an elevator to the third floor where her office was. And easy access to classrooms thanks to handicapped rulings. She could manage the ramp into the building where she taught. Worst case, she'd hire a student to push her.

Jake now thought it might be one of her students. But why? What did she have that they wanted?

Brianna was dressed and in the living room talking with Harvey Benson when Jake arrived shortly after noon. Martha Benson was still in the kitchen cleaning up after a delicious lunch that Brianna was happy to eat. Martha had also brought a cane she'd had to assist Brianna in becoming more mobile. Because of her wrist, she couldn't use crutches, but the cane helped immensely.

She met Jake at the door, proud to be on her own two feet.

He took in the situation with a quick glance, then

leaned over to brush a light kiss on her lips.

"I thought the doctor told you to stay off that foot for two days. Is this how you obey?" he said as he shut the front door behind him.

"Hello detective. I'm afraid I'm the guilty one here," Martha said, coming into the room still wiping her hands on a dishcloth. "I brought the cane. For when she's ready."

"I'm right here," Brianna said. "And I can't give into being an invalid. I have things to do!"

She'd been so proud of getting around and Jake was acting as if she'd committed a crime.

"I have some more sandwiches and soup, if you're hungry," Martha said after her husband had greeted Jake. "Did you already have lunch?"

"No I didn't. You're a life saver."

She beamed and turned back to the small kitchen. "Sit at the table, I'll bring it right out."

Jake shrugged out of his jacket, tossed it on the back of a chair and went to sit at the table. Brianna followed and sat opposite him.

Truth to tell, she was glad to get off her foot. Maybe she was rushing it a bit trying to be more mobile.

"This looks terrific," he said when Martha brought in a plate piled high with freshly made sandwiches and a steaming bowl of vegetable soup.

"I guess she took one look at your size and figured you needed plenty to keep going," Brianna murmured looking at the food in front of Jake.

"You eat half. You're too skinny."

"I ate plenty just a little while ago."

"You've lost weight in the past two years. Were you pining away for love?" he asked sardonically.

"You have a mean streak in you," she said, withdrawing slightly. "Just because you don't believe in love, doesn't mean others don't."

"You're too smart and have too much going for you to waste away for love."

"You've got that right. I'm going ahead with my life!"

He sat back in his chair, watching her, amusement dancing in his eyes. "How are you going to do that?"

Haughtily she lifted her eyebrow. "I don't believe that is any concern of yours. You made that perfectly clear. Did you bring home the class listings?"

"Yes." He went over to the chair, reached inside his jacket and withdrew a thick computer printout. He handed it to her.

"Good grief, I never knew I had that many students," she was surprised at how many pages were in the stack.

"These are for all your classes last year and the year before, as well as last semester."

"I wouldn't count the current students. The first break-in happened over the Christmas break. Why would one of those students want to break in?"

"Why would any of them want to?" He resumed eating his lunch. "Tell me what you know about each one."

She scanned the list for the first class. "You know, Jake, we can narrow this down right away by eliminating the women and short men. I mean, the guy on the steps was taller than I am, so that would eliminate anyone under five-nine. And we know it was a man, right?"

"Cross them off." He tossed her a pen.

Brianna read through the list, crossing off the women, pausing now and then as she had to search her memory to bring an image to mind. It was slow going. Some names meant nothing to her. Others she remembered instantly. Rereading the list, she had to think about some of them. Jake finished and Martha whipped away the plates as if she'd been hovering around him ready to finish cleaning.

While Brianna was reviewing the list, he followed Martha into the kitchen.

"No trouble?" he asked.

"None at all," she replied.

"I appreciate you and your husband coming to stay with her. I'll be here the rest of the day."

"We'll get going then, soon as I have this kitchen to rights. You call on us if you need us again. Imagine someone breaking into a house in this neighborhood. Why I never heard of such a thing."

While Jake was in the kitchen, Brianna rose and limped to the sofa, sitting on the soft cushions to resume her reading.

She glanced at Harvey, reading a book.

"Thanks for taking good care of me, Harvey," she said with a sweet smile. "I think the next shift has arrived."

"Nothing to it, Brianna. But you won't need us old folks around when you have that young cop on hand. You call us if you need us again, you hear?"

"I will."

When the Bensons had left, Jake joined her on the sofa.

"Well?" he asked.

"I can't think of a reason for any of these kids to want to break into my house or car. Office, maybe, if it were finals time. But this all happened after finals. I don't think it's a student."

He shrugged. "It may not be. But I'm not ready to discount it. What about faculty? Anyone you aced out of a promotion or something?"

She thought about it for a moment. "Not that I know of, but when I was hired, I wasn't the only one competing for the position. But that's been a few years. Surely no one held a grudge that long."

He shrugged.

"Impasse. I'm as puzzled now as I was after the first break in."

"We'll find him. We just need a break somewhere."

Brianna looked over the list again.

"Why do some names have question marks?"

"I can't remember these kids at all. They may have registered but not completed the course."

"Can you cross check with grades?"

"Sure, but it'd be easier for the computer to do it. I can do that at my office."

"Not today."

"But I need to get back to work and can't have one of the town's detectives trailing me. You should be out there doing real criminal work, not trying to find some bozo out there looking for something I haven't a clue what."

"I told you, I took a few days off. And the man's elevated to a higher threat when he pushed you down the stairs."

"I need to get back to work. The semester's started and I have no lesson plans thanks to that guy."

"Okay, okay, I get it. It doesn't look like you're going to be a model patient, anyway," he said.

She grinned. "Oh, like guys are? I'll be ready soon. Help me up. And I'll use the wheelchair for the campus ride."

"At least you show some sense."

She ignored his muttered comment and limped in to get ready.

On the ride to the campus, Brianna remembered the reception. She looked at Jake, wondering what he'd say when she told him she wanted to go.

"There's a reception for a new computer science professor on Saturday evening. I'd like to go. It's always nice to welcome new professors and especially one that can help with computer work if needed."

"No." he said.

"Umm perhaps I phrased that incorrectly. On Saturday night I'm attending a reception for a new professor."

"Too risky."

"Then you come with me and be my bodyguard."

The seconds ticked by with agonized slowness. Finally she dared risk a peek into his face.

His was all hard angles and planes. His eyes were dark and fathomless, his expression remote. He glanced at her. "If we haven't found the man by then, I'll go. I don't want you going anywhere by yourself."

She nodded. Surely no one would risk something in public. So far every incident had been in the dark, or alone.

"Is it fancy?" he asked.

"No, a suit would be fine."

"I won't have anything to say at a gathering of university professors," he warned.

She smiled as she envisioned the normally academic event.

"I wouldn't worry about that if I were you. You won't have to say anything to the women. They'll fall all over themselves just to stand near you. You'll be hotter than Damon. And the men will be so anxious to prove that they're just as macho, they'll be ridiculous." She remembered one event when her brother Jase had been there. She wouldn't have believed it if she hadn't seen it for herself.

A dull flush spread on his cheeks and his eyes grew even darker.

Brianna was charmed at the reaction to her teasing. Not wanting to push her luck, however, she refrained from expanding on it. "If you turn here, you can access parking. "

He found a place not too far from her office building. Jake made quick work of parking and retrieving the wheel chair from the back. As he pushed her along the quiet walkways, he kept a sharp eye out for anything suspicious.

"Classes have started again."

"I can tell," he said as he dodged a group of students talking so much they didn't see him and the wheelchair.

Brianna moved from the wheel chair to her desk chair when they reached her small office. She turned on the computer and waited.

They'd passed several open office doors as others held office hours, or were in catching up.

"I think I'll be better able to do something if you stop watching my every move," she said, irritated when she began to pull up the rosters from past semesters. Jake watched her like she was going to fall over or something.

He glanced out the hall, and then nodded once. "I'll be back," he said and left.

As she'd suspected, when she cross checked the lists, there were quite a few students who had signed up for the course and then dropped. There were several withdrawals after the grading had started.

But none of the names rang a bell. She still had no idea who would target her this way.

Jake hadn't returned by the time she compared the lists, so she began once again putting down her overview of the lectures for the coming term. Next time she was saving everything to the cloud. Even if no one broke in again, her laptop could be damaged or crash. She'd been too complaisant.

It was mid afternoon when Jake showed up again. She looked up, feeling a little tired with all the mental work on top of trying to ignore the pain in her ankle and typing wasn't helping her wrist at all.

"You ready to blow this joint?" he asked.

"Yeah. Maybe there was something to that doctor's advice. Let me close this down."

"So you're not up to going shopping?"

She looked up. "For?"

"The things on the list for the cabin."

A bubble of anticipation rose. Her fatigue vanished. She hadn't meant to become so involved that she ended up shopping with him, but it beat staying home. And she'd make sure he got exactly what she'd envisioned. Make sure he bought the items to make his cabin the comfortable home he wanted. She could do that for him if nothing else.

In no time they were heading to the largest mall in town.

"This is nice of you to go to all this trouble. What can I do to pay you back?" Brianna asked.

"Do what you're told for a change," he replied.

"Of course, as long as what I'm told is what I want to do. But I promise to be totally agreeable this afternoon."

"That'll be a switch."

"I can be very agreeable. Just you watch."

He glanced over to her, noting her smug smile as she gazed out the windshield. She was always easy to be with, even when she was in a snit. He smiled slightly, wondering what her idea of being totally agreeable was. How far could he push her? It would be an interesting afternoon.

Brianna teased and flirted and enjoyed herself tremendously. From the first moment when they arrived in the mall, she decided to make the shopping venture memorable. She knew from her brothers that men did not like shopping. Her goal was to make sure Jake remembered this trip all his life.

Jake initially protested every suggestion she made. At first, Brianna started to grow annoyed, but by the third time, she realized he was teasing her. From then on, they grew more and more outrageous in their discussions about the curtains, rugs and other accessories for the cabin.

The poor saleswoman was bewildered and tried to be so diplomatic.

Twice, Brianna caught Jake's eye and they exchanged a secret smile at the obvious efforts of the saleswoman. In the end, they bought nearly everything on the list.

Giggling softly as he pushed the chair out into the open part of the mall, Brianna waited until they'd left the store before turning around to look at him.

"We were awful. That poor woman."

He matched her grin. "She got a hefty commission out of the final sale. She'll be fine. What were you doing arguing with me? I thought you were going to be totally agreeable."

"Jake, I was the one being reasonable. That purple rug you wanted for the bathroom was hideous!"

"It's my bathroom."

"And you probably would have given up showering if you had to face that every day."

"Want to stop for a cup of coffee?" He paused by a bakery that had small tables scattered around the opening.

Taking a deep breath of the fragrant air, Brianna nodded.

They took a table, moving one of the chairs so the wheel chair fit. The waitress quickly appeared, took their order and left.

He leaned back in his chair, all casual male animal. His long legs stretched out before him, he regarded her with a lazy, possessive air. "You're pretty when you get worked up about something," he said unexpectedly.

Brianna's breath caught in her throat. Her eyes widened and she stared at him. He carried himself with such a don't-give-a-damn attitude, he was almost scary. But she never feared him— only her own reactions and feelings around him.

Now watching him stare at her caused her heart to race. She wanted to fling herself into his lap and hold on for dear life. The image of their kisses the other night sprang into her mind. Unconsciously she licked her lips. His gaze was drawn to her mouth and slowly he sat up, reached over and brushed her damp lips with the pad of his thumb. Cupping her chin with his palm, he rubbed her lips again.

Brianna felt the touch to her toes. Every cell quivered to attention. Butterflies danced in her stomach. Her gaze was captured by his and she couldn't look away. She knew he'd see the love residing deep within her, but there was nothing she could do to conceal that. He already knew, so what did it matter?

He knew and it changed nothing.

"You're dangerous to be around." His voice was so low she had to strain to hear.

"Why?" A whisper only, but she hadn't the strength to speak aloud. Bonded to Jake by the touch of his hand, by the caress of his thumb, she clutched the arms of the wheelchair tightly to keep herself from throwing her arms around his neck. They were in a public place, for heaven's sake. She had to demonstrate a modicum of decorum.

"Because you get a man thinking things he has no business thinking. Wishing for things that aren't possible." He released her and sat back, breaking eye contact as he scanned the bakery, looking for their waitress. Spotting her walking toward them, he kept his eyes on her.

Brianna couldn't look away. What had he meant?

"Here you go, folks. A chocolate éclair, a brownie and two cups of coffee." Placing the order on the table, the waitress smiled and turned away.

Brianna didn't want the sweet. She wanted to go home. She wanted them to be alone, where he could kiss her as if there was no tomorrow.

"Change your mind?" he asked as she continued to stare at him, ignoring the éclair.

"Let's go home," she said, her voice husky with emotion.

His eyes locked on hers. Long moments slowly passed.

"No," he said briefly.

She broke contact and reached for her fork. The éclair tasted like chalk. But she ate every bit of it. The coffee warmed her. She hadn't realized how chilled she'd grown.

Finally finished, she idly glanced around the bakery. The brightness of the day had faded. She was getting tired. Maybe she should go home and take a nap.

"Tomorrow I'm going to work," she said, not looking at him.

"If you feel up to it."

"I do. But I'm tired now. We've gotten most of the things on the list. Can we go home? I want to take a nap before dinner."

She remembered from two years ago that sleep helped when she was depressed. It afforded an escape and for the moment was what she wanted most.

"I still need to get some pictures."

"Another time, Jake. I'm tired." She refused to meet his eyes.

Brianna went straight to bed when she reached home. She slept until dinner, ate, then returned to her room. Reading, she tried to quell all thoughts of Jake until she finally fell asleep.

The next morning, she dressed and was ready to leave for the campus in time for her first class. She didn't speak as he drove her. The wheelchair had been left behind and she was relying on the cane. Her ankle was better today and her wrist barely ached.

"I'll walk you to class," he said, pulling the car to a halt before the Tadlow Building. He put a placard in the window denoting law enforcement and came to open her door.

"Thank you." She didn't want to admit she was just a bit nervous. Not that she was carrying anything anyone would want today, only her shoulder bag. Still, it would take a while for the uncertainty to fade.

Jake not only walked her to her room, he sat in the back during the class, studying the students, watching Brianna.

"You didn't have to wait," she said after the last student had left at the end of the hour.

"I only had a couple of math courses in college. My major was criminology. But if I'd taken one of yours, I might have signed up for more. You make it sound so exciting, as if it's the greatest subject in the world," he said, ignoring her comment.

"I like it," she said stiffly.

"It shows. And you make it come alive for these kids. I loved your example about the cattle ranch."

"So much of math is practical, but people don't always realize it."

"So you make sure they do."

She nodded, pleased he liked her teaching technique.

"I shouldn't be surprised. You bring a lot of enthusiasm to everything you do," he said thoughtfully.

"For the most part, life is wild and wonderful. Why not express it?"

"Yeah, why not? Where to next?"

"I have a break for an hour, then another class. You really don't have to hang around."

"I want to," he said simply.

Jake stayed with her all day Wednesday and Thursday. Friday was a free day, and she had him drop her off at her office and then leave. She needed to get caught up on all the administrative work involved with her job as well as redo the lost lesson plans. And she needed to do it alone. He was too distracting.

Saturday he was gone most of the day. She longed to ask where he was going, but kept quiet. It was enough that he thought the danger had diminished by asking Mrs. Benson to stay with her. That woman would not be a match for the man in the stairwell. But nothing had happened in the last several days. Maybe the guy realized she didn't have what he wanted and he'd moved on.

By six-thirty she was ready for the reception. She took off the bandage pleased the worst of the bruise and scrape was fading. The dress she chose was a warm, light woolen one, pale cream with a blue pattern that caught the color of her eyes. She had no choice of footwear, a flat pump for her right foot and a walking cast on her injured left foot.

Mrs. Bensen let Jake in when he arrived. Brianna walked into the living room when she heard him. He looked gorgeous. The dark charcoal gray suit with a crisp white shirt and red tie made the perfect escort for the reception.

"Wow," she said softly,

He frowned. "You ready?"

She smiled and nodded slowly. "I think I'm changing my mind."

"Why?"

"Because one look at you and everyone else will forget the guest of honor."

"Right. I'll give it a miss if you want."

For a moment, she gave serious thought to staying home and spend the evening just the two of them.

"Nonsense, she's spent effort getting ready. You two

go and have fun," Martha said, putting on her old jacket. "Good night, and have fun."

She left and Brianna smiled.

"She's right, I really should attend. It's good form, you know. And when I make professor, I want everyone to come to my party."

"Invite me when that event occurs. I'll come," he said, holding her heavy coat for her. He fastened it, ending with the button beneath her chin. Cupping her chin, he raised her face for a light kiss.

The reception was in full swing when they arrived. Brianna greeted members of her department who were concerned about her recovery. Jake had his arm around her waist, half-holding her to minimize the weight on her ankle. She introduced him to everyone as they greeted others she knew.

"Find a chair and sit. I'll get you a drink," he said, scanning the room.

"Every time we go anywhere, you check the place out as if you're expecting a gang of terrorists. It's creepy," she said, gladly sitting at one of the small tables on the edge of the large room near a favorite fellow professor.

Gerald Holcomb greeted her and sat beside her. One of the long-term professors in the mathematics department, Brianna was glad to have someone to talk to.

"Can I get you something to drink?" Jake asked both Brianna and the professor.

Brianna took a soft drink merely to keep a straight head on her shoulders. She considered this still a business meeting.

"I'm set," Professor Holcomb said, raising a glass still full.

To Brianna's surprise, Jake returned with a drink for each of them. He sat on another chair at the table and listened to the conversation between Gerald and herself about new programs expected for freshmen. Jake gave no indication he wanted to move an inch.

She wondered once or twice if he'd be bored with the conversation. It tended so often to gravitate toward university concerns.

Probably cops talk shop when they got together, too.

"...two errors, which I quickly corrected. Computers are fine, but only as accurate as the person entering the data," Gerald Holcomb was saying.

"Sorry, I missed the first part," Brianna said. She needed to pay attention, not be worried if Jake was enjoying himself.

"I said I compared the computer-generated grade sheet with my own records and found two errors. Not that one student would have minded. His score and the others were reversed. It pays to double-check. Don't you agree, Brianna?"

"Yes, I do, actually. I've never found an error. Did the grades from last semester get posted?"

"They were in the mail last week, Wednesday or Thursday, I think. I know I checked over the weekend."

Brianna gave Jake a telling glance.

"My briefcase was stolen with the mail in it."

"I heard. Sorry about all that. You can get you a duplicate."

"Actually, I don't have my notes, either. My office was broken into and trashed. When I got everything squared away, my lesson plans, final exams and grades were missing. I didn't worry about it too much because I'd already turned in my grades."

Jake leaned over. "Tell me about the grading system. You send in the grades, the administration department keys them into a computer, then sends you a listing to verify accuracy?"

Professor Holcomb nodded. "That's right. The grades have already been posted, but it never hurts to double-check. If there are errors, we can catch them. As I did with these two young men."

"Brianna, were you missing your grades for your fall classes?"

She nodded. "My grade book was stolen. But it didn't matter since I had already turned in my grades."

"Could they be changed?"

"I don't see how."

"Hackers can get into any computer," Gerald said. "In fact, I believe those focusing in computer science almost consider it a rite of passage to break into the college computers. Usually they leave trick reports easily flagged as not real. But in my case, one of the students changed the grades."

Jake looked at Brianna. "Could someone have changed your grades in the college computer? Someone who then made sure you couldn't double-check?"

"It's possible," Gerald Holcomb said before Brianna

could answer.

She nodded. It was possible.

"Tomorrow we get a copy of the grades and you see which ones you remember. If any are glaringly different, we'll have a starting point," Jake said.

"Good grief, Jake. I had over a hundred and fifty students. I can't remember what grade each one earned."

"It's worth looking at."

"I say, is this detective work?" Professor Holcomb asked excitedly.

Brianna turned back to Gerald, exasperated. "Yes. I wanted to enjoy the reception, not think about this. Apparently policemen never leave their work."

"One of the hazards of the job," Jake murmured.

"You're off duty tonight, detective. Enjoy yourself."

"I am." His smiled at her and her heart began to race.

Nine

“I always wanted to be a detective. I remember once when I was a young man…”

Brianna tuned out Gerald’s ramblings and let her gaze drift around the room, but she couldn’t concentrate on anything but Jake. Blast! She wished to give the appearance of being totally oblivious to him. If he guessed how he affected her, would his attentions escalate?

He’d made it clear more than once that he wasn’t interested. At least not interested in what she wanted.

Yet he continued to touch her, kiss her. He easily conversed with the professor and others who came by their table to greet her, not wanting her to have to stand on her injured ankle.

Now his fingers seemed to have developed a will of their own. How could he calmly converse with the professor when his threaded through hers and focused her full attention on him? Her heartbeat was loud enough to be heard across the room.

She was grateful when Susan Talbot joined them. At least Jake stood then and offered his seat, breaking contact, giving Brianna breathing room.

"I'm so pleased to meet you, Detective. We all wondered who Brianna brought with her. She usually comes to these things alone. But when I heard you were the one investigating the assault, well, I just had to come meet you and tell you we would all do anything to help."

Susan was of average height, yet next to Jake she looked almost petite. Her dark hair was cut short, her brown eyes were deep and sultry as she flirted provocatively.

Brianna gritted her teeth. "Your mistake, Susan. Jake is not handling the investigation. He and I are longtime friends."

Jake glanced at her, his expression carefully neutral. Thoughtfully he nodded and turned back to Susan. "Brianna and I go back quite a while. Do you teach in the mathematics department, as well?"

"Oh, no, I'm in anthro." Susan smiled flirtatiously and then looked at Brianna. "You don't mind if I take Jake and introduce him to everyone? I know you're fairly immobile with that ankle. We'll be right back." Tucking her hand into his arm, she drew him across the room. Brianna was not so pleased with Susan after all. Not that she betrayed her emotions by even a flicker of her eyelids. For a moment, she watched to see how he fit in, meeting so many men and women from the college.

The two life-styles were so different. Would he feel out of place?

Slowly Brianna stood, leaning on the cane Martha had lent her. "Gerald, I'd like to mingle a bit. Would you walk around with me?"

She refused to watch Jake any longer. He was a

grown man and he could fend for himself. And she needed to fend for herself.

Brianna congratulated Professor Sorenson on his promotion and met the new professor.

She answered endless questions about her fall and the break-in of her office. She didn't tell everyone about her house and car. Speculation and gossip were rampant enough without that.

It was clear everyone else thought, as Susan Standford had, that Jake was accompanying her for protection, and that he was investigating the case. It was an obvious conclusion.

He was a policeman and she had not brought another man to any university affairs in over two years. When they'd been dating, she had been reluctant to share their time together. And then once he'd stopped calling, she hadn't wanted to spend her time with any other men.

She limped slowly across the reception hall. Stopping beside Jake, she smiled at the small group discussing the latest science fiction film. He glanced at her, smiled and slipped his arm around her waist. Gratefully, Brianna leaned against him.

When she was asked about the film, she had to reply, "I haven't seen it yet."

She rarely went to the movies. She didn't like going alone.

"We could go tomorrow," Jake murmured softly.

"I thought you've seen it," she said, warmed by the offhand invitation.

"I wouldn't mind seeing it again. Then I could see if Tyler's assessment of the hidden social implications is accurate."

"It is, Jake. Would I lead anyone astray?" The young assistant professor of sociology grinned engagingly.

"Put it down to my suspicious nature. Cops like to investigate things on their own," Jake responded.

He looked at Brianna again. Taking in how tired she looked.

"We've got to be going. It's been a pleasure." He eased her away from the group and toward the door.

She walked beside him, leaning on him a bit more than earlier. Her ankle hurt, her wrist ached and her head had begun to pound.

"You look exhausted." He got her coat, slipped it on her and tilted up her face. "Have you visited enough?"

"Yes. It's more tiring than I expected. At this rate, I won't' be good for anything for weeks."

"You don't want to force it or you can put back your recovery."

"Thank you, *Dr. Morgan,* for your expert medical assessment of the situation."

"Mouthy." He brushed his lips over hers, which effectively shut her up.

Brianna wanted to look around to see who might have noticed, but she dared not. Better to ignore the gesture and leave with some dignity. She hoped everyone in the room was too busy with their own conversations to notice Jake's kiss.

In less than ten minutes, Jake pulled his car up in front of Brianna's house. When he opened her door, he did not give her the chance to step out, but reached in and scooped her up.

"Jake! I can walk."

"You're tired. It's a short way to the house." By the time he finished talking, he'd reached her front stoop. Setting her gently on her feet, he waited as she found her key. Taking it from her cold fingers, he inserted it and opened the door. Gently he urged her inside and closed the door behind them.

"I enjoyed meeting the people you work with on a social level," he said.

"Still think one of them is trying to steal my article idea?" she asked, shrugging out of her coat. She steadied herself against the wall. She was more tired than she realized.

"No. But talking with Gerald has given me another lead to check out. First thing Monday, I'm going to get a list of all your students' grades from last semester and we're going over them to see if any have been altered."

"Like I'm going to remember exactly what each student earned," she complained. "My grade book had all that information."

"It's a starting place. Do you need any help getting to bed?"

She shook her head.

"Tomorrow we can still find the movie at a theater in town."

"Oh, you don't have to take me. I can wait for it to come out on video."

"We made a date. I have witnesses," he said whimsically.

She smiled. "Okay, I would like to see it. I'll be ready at three."

He reached out and drew her into his arms. Brianna gave a sigh and raised her face. Suddenly her zipper slid down, the cool air startling against her skin.

"Jake!"

"Relax, Brie. I'm just helping. This looked awkward to unfasten with your wrist." He released the fasteners of her bra.

Daring images danced in her mind. She could imagine herself slipping her arms from the dress, letting it trail down her body as Jake watched. Desire flooded her. She'd loved him for so long. Slowly she raised her face to his, letting that love shine from her eyes.

"Look at me like that and I won't be responsible for what I might do," he said in a husky tone.

"Maybe I don't care," she replied in a whisper.

Stepping closer, she reached up to encircle his neck. The cool air on her back contrasted with the burning heat wherever she pressed against Jake. She felt his warm hands on her bare skin and shivered. She felt feminine and soft. Angling her mouth, she lifted her lips for a kiss.

A muffled groan escaped Jake as he hugged her so tightly against him she couldn't breathe.

She feasted on the embrace as if it was ambrosia. His taste was achingly familiar, wildly exciting. The embrace gave her a precious sense of safety and security.

The flames licking throughout her contrasted to that security. They were dangerous, daring and demanding. She wanted more. More of Jake, more of the love that she felt so strongly.

Jake eased back, his eyes opening to gaze down into hers. Resting his forehead against hers, he almost felt he could drown in the blue eyes that beckoned so enticingly.

Her lips were moist and rosy, still parted as if she would resume the kiss. He felt like he'd been kicked.

Tenderly he pulled back, cupped her face, rubbing gently over her lips, feeling the dampness on his thumb.

"This is not a good idea, Brie."

"It feels good to me," she said softly, her hand threaded in his thick hair. She could feel the pounding of his heart against hers. It matched the tempo of her own.

"Your brother was right. I'm not the man for you."

"My brother? What brother? What are you talking about?"

She pulled back and stared at him, confused. When had either of her brothers even met Jake, much less spoken to him?

What *was* he talking about?

"Never mind." He straightened, his expression instantly remote, forbidding. "If you can get yourself to bed all right, I'll get my change of clothes from the car and bunk down in here. Go to bed."

Not waiting for her to say a word, he left and headed for his car. He closed the door behind him relishing the icy air that shocked him back into awareness. No more kissing!

He'd blown it. He'd never wanted her to know.

Not that she knew anything. But he didn't want her curiosity to force a confrontation.

He would not let his guard down for a second. He couldn't wait until they'd reviewed the grade sheets. If there was a student whose grades were changed, they'd have another lead.

If not, he'd turn the entire investigation back to Don Winston.

Don was the officer of record. He should be doing the work.

Jake sat in the car until the lights went off inside. He still had her key and let himself quietly back in to the house. He wondered why he didn't just turn the investigation back to Don immediately. He could handle things.

And Jake feared he might not be able to handle his own feelings much longer.

Brianna heard Jake return. She was tempted to get up and confront him, but she wasn't sure about what.

Exactly what had Jake meant with the comment about her brother? Which one? Jase? Josh? To her knowledge, neither had met Jake. Something didn't make sense.

Tomorrow she'd demand some answers. He couldn't casually slip something like that into a conversation and then blow it off.

Sleep proved evasive. Which brother had told Jake he was not the man for her? And why? How could Jake have bought into such an idea? Was that why he stopped seeing her?

He was not the only one looking for answers tomorrow. And hers had nothing to do with grades and students.

One look at Jake's face the next morning, however, and Brianna knew she wasn't going to get a quick answer to her questions.

She'd dressed warmly with dark wool slacks that

hugged her hips and a pink sweater that she loved.

"Can you access grades from your computer at your office?" he asked before she'd even had coffee.

"Yes. Can we eat first?"

"Let's go out to breakfast, check out the records and catch the early matinee for the movie," he suggested, already reaching for his jacket.

Today he was dressed in jeans and a thick sweater. She didn't know if she liked him better in a suit as a detective or jeans as the man she loved.

He helped her on with her jacket, his knuckles brushing against her jaw.

She reached up to flip out her hair, trying to match his casual attitude. Her skin tingled where he'd touched her. Her heart raced, and breathing became a chore.

His hand brushed over the shiny waves, lingering on the ends as he rubbed them gently between his fingers.

She didn't bring up the question in the forefront of her mind, though her curiosity almost spiked out of control. She glanced at her watch wondering if either brother would be around a phone at nine o'clock on a Sunday morning.

They had breakfast at a restaurant Brianna hadn't eaten at before. It was near Jake's home and she suspected he'd eaten there more than once from the familiarity he had with the menu.

The campus was quieter than on a normal school day, but there were still students around and other teachers in their offices.

She perused the grades from last semester. Nothing seemed extraordinary. But with so many students, and the loss of her own grading book, she wasn't one hundred percent certain no grades had been altered.

Before she left her office, on one of Jake's surveillance rounds, she tried calling her brothers. Jase's phone went to voice mail. Josh's didn't ring at all. She tried Shannon's, but her phone just rang and rang. Where were they?

Brianna and Jake headed for the early matinee at the movie theater downtown.

To Brianna's surprise Tyler Hunter and a young woman were in the lobby buying popcorn. Once they spotted Jake and Brianna, he left her in line and hurried over.

"I heard you plan to come today, and thought I'd take a chance you'd be at this matinee. We're going to see the movie with you. That way I can point out the social aspects I was discussing last night," Tyler boomed heartily.

They walked to the line where he quickly introduced Liza Nesbet, his girlfriend.

Brianna smiled politely, wishing she and Jake had gone to a different theater or at a different showing. She didn't want to share Jake with these two acquaintances.

She had planned on the two of them spending the afternoon together. And maybe the evening. She wasn't going to let the day go by without finding out what he'd meant by that statement he'd let slip last night.

"Popcorn, no butter, and a cherry cola?" Jake asked Brianna as they stepped up to the counter. His hand was warm against the small of her back.

As she turned slightly to smile up at him, it felt

almost as if he were embracing her, his arm touching her shoulders, her back, his hand firmly guiding her.

She nodded. He remembered. After two years and who knew how many other women, he remembered what she liked at the movies. For a second, she wished it meant something.

Feeling inexplicably better, Brianna resigned herself to a shared afternoon. But later, she'd get Jake alone and question him about that curious statement he'd made.

The movie was fun. Despite her earlier misgivings, Brianna enjoyed Tyler's comments and the rude retorts his girlfriend made to put down his pretensions. They complemented each other, and at one point Brianna wondered what they thought of her and Jake. Did they appear to complement one another?

He sat beside her, but made no move to hold her hand or put his arm around her shoulders. He held the popcorn in his lap, and she snuggled closer, ostensibly to better reach the snack.

Mingling with the aroma of the freshly popped corn was Jake's own scent, tangy and masculine, uniquely his.

She longed to dash the bag from his hand, knock over the drinks and crawl into his lap. Did anyone ever do that in the movie theater? Would she be starting a trend? Or causing a scandal? She could see the headlines in the local paper—Math Professor Shocks Theatergoers With Wanton Behavior.

She sighed and reached for some more popcorn. It would never happen, but she wished she dared.

Tyler and Liza suggested stopping together for a snack when the movie was over.

Because they ate breakfast late, and only had popcorn during the movie, Jake raised an eyebrow at Brianna in silent inquiry.

"Sure," she said, not at all interested, but didn't want to be rude to Tyler and Liza.

Jake suggested a grill down on Third Street. "It's a cop hangout, but I think you'd like it," he explained, glancing down at Brianna.

Saying nothing, she nodded. Two years ago, he hadn't taken her to any cop hangouts. They had gone to dinner in nice restaurants, cooked at her house. But he'd never taken her where his coworkers hung out. Why now?

Jake was well liked. That much was evident from the men and women who greeted him when he walked into the grill. Several came over to visit briefly when they were seated. Tyler and Liza joined in the conversation as if they'd been longtime friends with everyone, and more and more chairs were dragged up, crowding their table. Brianna said very little, watching the activity. Jake deliberately put up barriers. Why?

When a pert and friendly red-haired woman joined them, Jake introduced her as Diane Waters. Brianna's attention immediately focused on the woman. This was Diane? Jake's date for New Year's Eve? She was adorable.

Gritting her teeth, Brianna wanted to disappear. She didn't need this.

At the first break in the conversation, she glared at Jake. "I have a headache. Do you think you could take me home and then come back?"

"Have something to eat first. It'll make you feel better."

"The service here isn't the greatest, but the food's hearty," Diane said genially. She leaned over Jake and hugged him. "I haven't seen you for a while. Where've you been? Up at your cabin?"

He nodded. "Fixing it up some."

"When do I get to see it?" she asked, her bright, bubbly enthusiasm almost more than Brianna could bear.

She stood up and excused herself, first heading toward the bathroom, then veering to the front door and outside.

Once on the sidewalk, she looked down the street. It was too far to walk home, she knew she couldn't with her ankle. And she'd left her jacket on the back of the chair inside. Otherwise she might try it. The wind blew from the west, chilling her to the bone. She pulled her phone from her purse—

"What the hell do you think you're doing?" Jake asked, pulling her around, clamping his hands on her shoulders in a hard grip. His eyes blazing down on her.

"I'm going home. I told you I had a headache."

"If you would eat something besides popcorn, you'll feel better."

"When I need a mother, I'll let you know. I want to go home." She knew she sounded childish, but she couldn't help it. She just wanted to be away from this place, away from his friends, away from Diane.

"Too good for the grill? These people not intellectuals like college professors?

She blinked at the comment, staring up at him. Was

that really how he interpreted her actions?

"It's not that," she said, suddenly feeling guilty. She really hadn't given them a chance. Mainly she didn't want to be around Diane. It was too painful.

"It sure looks like it. Where are your manners? Certainly you can bear up long enough to eat. After all, Tyler and Liza are here. They're from your world. Talk to them if that makes you feel any better."

"It's not that," she mumbled. Her gaze dropped to his chin. She couldn't tell him. Yet she didn't want him to think she was such a snob that she didn't like his friends and co-workers.

"What is it, then?" He leaned over until his nose almost touched hers, his hand beneath her chin, tilting her face to meet his. "If it isn't that, what is it?"

She didn't want to have to say it. It made her seem so petty. But it was true.

"I'm jealous," she whispered.

"What?" He stared at her for a long moment. "Are you nuts?"

She shook her head, embarrassment flooding her.

He cupped her chin and his thumb caressed her jaw. She hated looking at him, afraid of the disgust she'd see or the laughter.

But she saw only confusion.

"Why are you jealous? Or is the question who are you jealous of?"

"Whom."

"Brianna."

"Diane."

He stared down at her for long moments. The wind

whipped around them, cold and harsh. Brianna didn't feel it. The heat of embarrassment threatened to consume her.

She didn't want to feel this way. He'd made it clear there was no future in a relationship between them. And he was certainly free to see anyone he wanted.

But she felt raw with jealousy. She bitterly resented the fact he had invited Diane to spend New Year's Eve with him. Bitterly resented the fact he'd been dating while she had been so lonely since he'd gone. Bitterly resented the fact she loved a man who didn't love her in return.

"Diane is a friend. She works in dispatch and sometimes we go out. Just for fun. There's no need for you to be jealous of her or anyone else." His voice was soft and husky.

"Jake?" Tyler peered around the door. Laughter and light spilled from the opening. "Is everything okay?"

"Yes. The cold air cured her headache. We're coming back in now," Jake said, his eyes never leaving Brianna's.

"The waiter's finally ready to take our orders."

"We'll be right there."

The door closed and they were alone on the sidewalk again.

"Coming?" he asked softly.

"What, refuse to return and make a cop out to be a liar?" she asked. Her heart ached, but there appeared to be nothing to do but go on with the evening.

Brianna was relieved to find Diane had left the group by the time she and Jake returned. Once the early dinner arrived, the others drifted away until only the four of them remained at their table. Despite the rocky beginning, she relaxed and began to enjoy herself. Tyler and Liza were a funny couple, had been together for several months and were discussing marriage. This was from Tyler—Liza kept flirting with him, yet holding him off.

When she and Brianna went to the rest room at one point, Liza admitted she was crazy for the guy. "But I don't want him to become too complacent—even after we marry. How will he appreciate me if I fall too easily?"

Brianna nodded, but wondered if she could ever play games like that. She would want her husband as secure in her love as she would wish to be in his.

When they finished eating, Jake asked if she wanted to leave. She shook her head. She was having fun.

Again the numbers at the table swelled. Tyler was in seventh heaven, arguing social problems with cynical policemen. Jake leaned back and watched Brianna discussing the current college art exhibit with Sergeant Leroy Burns. Leroy's hobby was oil painting and he and Brianna compared reactions to the exhibit.

It was late when they left.

"I liked your friends," she said with a yawn as he settled her in the car.

"Good."

She was pleasantly tired. The evening had turned out much better than she had thought at the beginning. Diane had not reappeared and that helped.

When Jake stopped the car at her place, she rolled her head against the back of the seat and looked at him.

"Which brother did you talk to and what did you

two discuss?" she asked. She couldn't let the evening end without knowing. She suspected it might be important.

"Drop it, Brie. It's old news and changes nothing."

"Jake, I want to know," she insisted.

He opened his door and walked around to open hers. "Sometimes we don't always get what we want," he said as he helped her out onto the sidewalk. "Give me your keys and let's get inside. It's cold."

She went to her room and tried both brothers again. Jase answered on the third ring.

"Hey," Brianna said.

"What's up?" Jase asked.

She debated telling him about the break ins and the fall down the stairs, but decided against it. He'd only worry and she couldn't have better protection than Jake.

"I have a question for you and for Josh. Haven't reached him so you're first."

"About?"

She heard Shannon murmuring in the background.

"Did you ever meet Jake Morgan?"

"Who is he, someone at the college?"

"No he's a cop."

"Why do you know a cop?"

"It's a long story and starts almost three years ago. Do you or do you not know him?"

"Nope. Does he ride rodeos?"

"Hardly." She thought a moment. That only left Josh. What had he done?

"Know anything about Josh challenging a man I was dating?"

"Nope. Was it the cop?"

"I'll know once I talk to Josh. How's Shannon doing?"

Her new sister in law was already pregnant and both she and her brother were delighted.

"Good, want to talk to her?"

"Yes, I do."

Brianna told some of the situation to Shannon, with the warning not to tell Jase. Then asked about how the early stages of pregnancy were going. Except for morning sickness, Shannon was feeling great.

When their conversation ended, Brianna debated going back to the living room with Jake, but was too frustrated with Jake's refusal to answer her question. She knew she could question him from now until the cows came home, and if he chose not to respond, he wouldn't.

"There are always ways to find things out, Mr. Hotshot Detective. You are not the only one who can interrogate people. If you won't tell me, I'll find out from the source."

She tried Josh again. No answer. Where was he?

Jake drove the next morning, placed a police emblem on his dash and parked in her slot at the college. He walked her to class and sat in the back, alternating watching Brianna and the students.

When class was over, the students filed out. A young man entered the room and went to where Brianna was packing up her papers.

"Can I talk to you, professor?" the man asked.

"What's up?" she asked.

Jake came to the front of the room and stood to one side—alert and ready, but not interfering.

"I uh, thought, I uh, would get a better grade. I aced the midterm and the final. Did I uh, miss any assignments or something? I uh, got a C and I really expected an A."

She glanced at Jake. "Which class?"

"Calculus, Tuesdays and Thursdays. Umm, my friend Janey Howell did better than a C, too."

"You're Jim Smithers, right?"

He nodded.

"Did you hear my grade book was stolen?"

He nodded. "Does that mean nothing can be changed?"

"No, it means something is definitely wrong and you might be the clue to what it is. Do you have time to come to my office?"

"Sure." He glanced at Jake.

"He'll come, too," Brianna said.

She pulled up the grades for last fall's calculus class. Slowly she reviewed the grades again, trying to picture each student, trying to remember what the grades have been.

"I have my tests if you want to see them," Jim said, pulling a bunch out of his backpack and offered them.

Brianna reviewed them quickly remembering how well this student had grasped the class.

"Who is Margaret Albert?"

"That's Peggy," Jim said.

"Wait a minute. This is wrong. Peggy Albert failed the course. Yet this printout shows a C. I know she failed because she's on a scholarship and I hated to have to give a failing grade, but she didn't do the work and failed all the tests. Her final exam score was higher than anything she'd done all year, but not enough to raise the grade."

"So three students that you can remember now have different grades. Two lower than you remember, one higher," Jake summarized, looking over her shoulder.

She nodded, studying the lists. "Why didn't I see this yesterday?" Frustrated not to have her grade book, she tried to recall what each student had earned. Shaking her head in defeat, she looked up. "That's the best I can do. Where are the lists I sent into administration?"

"According to the woman I talked with in Administration, they keep them for a week after they send the grades out, then toss them. The theory is the professors still have the list of grades if any conflicts arise."

"Well, the college would be swamped with paper if it kept every piece," she said reasonably.

He stood and took the list she'd marked. "I'll give these to Don. He can start checking. We'll start with these two girls."

"Neither are as tall as I am. I can't see either one as the person on the stairs."

"I'll let you know if we turn anything up." He sketched her a small salute and headed for the elevators.

She smiled at Jimmy. "I'll make sure we correct this. I don't know what happened or how, but I can correct your grade. I appreciate your coming forward."

"Thank you, Professor." He nodded his head and

left.

Could those two girls, with help, have changed the grades? What other classes might be affected?

She called the administration office and discussed the situation with one of the women who could help her. Satisfied all was being done, Brianna called her friend Susan. She had a brother to see.

The sun hovered on the horizon by the time Susan and Brianna turned onto the long road that led to the Rafter C.

Jase had convinced her he truly hadn't a clue who Jake was.

That left Josh. Suspecting her bossy brother had interfered when he had no business being involved, she decided to confront him face-to-face rather than try to nail him down over the phone.

She didn't want to drive, so enlisted her friend Susan.

It had been several months since she'd been home and she felt the same surge of homecoming and delight she always felt when on the Rafter C.

You could take the girl off the ranch, but you couldn't take the ranch out of the girl. No matter how much she enjoyed teaching, she always felt at home here. Suddenly she was anxious for summer to return. She usually spent a few weeks in July riding, helping with the chores, renewing herself.

Josh was out when they arrived. It would be dark in another hour. He'd be back by then. Susan had visited before, and knew the layout of the house. She parked in back and they entered through the kitchen.

Brianna shook her head at the mess on the counters and in the sink. Since their former housekeeper had left to care of her invalid mother, Josh had not been able to keep a replacement.

And if anyone needed someone else to do housekeeping chores, it was her brother!

Susan giggled. "Typical bachelor, right? I can clean up."

"My family, my mess," Brianna said.

"You sit. Your wrist isn't fully healed and you need to stay off the foot as much as you can.

"Tell me more about Jake," Susan invited as she began running warm water into the sink. She'd been Brianna's confident when Jake had stopped coming around and wanted to know all the latest now.

"Brianna! I didn't know you were coming."

Josh entered the kitchen two hours later. Tall and lean, he looked tired and dusty. Shedding his shearling jacket and cowboy hat, he gave his sister a quick hug, and greeted Susan. When he glanced around the kitchen, his face lit up in a genuine smile.

"Thanks for cleaning up. And—" he drew in a deep breath "—from the tantalizing aroma coming from the oven, I'd say I'm more than glad you two came by. What did you fix?"

"Susan made meat loaf. You didn't have anything else. When are you going to get another housekeeper?"

"I'm working on it. Is it my fault none of the ones the local agency sends out will stay? Who wants to come to work on a remote ranch in the dead of winter? The last one only left a couple of days ago. I'll get someone soon. What's the occasion for the visit? What's happened? How did you get hurt?" he asked, spotting the support on her ankle.

"It's a long story. I'll tell you over dinner." And get a few answers in exchange!

Ten

They fell into a familiar routine. Susan served up dinner; Josh handed the silverware to Brianna to set the table. He brought the plates to the table from the kitchen. It reminded Brianna of evenings when she was growing up after her parents had died.

For so long it had just been Josh, Jase and her. The three against the world.

She didn't want her brother to have done anything that would alter their relationship. Glancing at Josh, she hesitated, then decided to withhold her questions until after they ate. No sense in ruining the meal Susan had prepared. Time enough for indigestion when they were finished.

As they began to eat, she explained how she had hurt her ankle.

"And the police haven't found out who did it yet?" he said, scowling.

She smiled at his expression, it was so similar to Jake's. While her brother had the same fair hair and light eyes that she had, his features were rugged and masculine. And he was just as quick to jump to her defense as Jake.

"They're working on it. They think they'll find the man soon."

"You should move back home until they do," he said firmly.

Susan looked at him. "No."

"My home's in Texarkana these days," Brianna said, trying to keep the sudden annoyance under control. She wasn't Josh's baby sister anymore—she was all grown up.

"Someone should be watching out for you."

"Get real. I'll look after myself."

"Don't seem to have done such a great job," he said, looking at her ankle.

Where had she gone wrong that she gave the men in her life the impression she couldn't take care of herself? Did all sisters go through this? she wondered.

"Someone's looking out for me," she replied.

"Someone special." Susan said with a grin.

Josh looked between them. "Someone new?" he asked, putting down his fork to study his sister.

"No. No one special. Actually, no one at all."

"What do you mean?" He pushed away his empty plate and stared at her, puzzled.

"I mean, I haven't been seeing anyone at all in more than two years."

"Oops," Susan said. She picked up her plate and Brianna's empty one, stacking them and heading for the kitchen. "I'll just see to these," she muttered leaving the brother and sister staring at each other.

Josh leaned back in his chair, his eyes never leaving hers. "Two years?"

"Uh-huh. Two years. Shall I tell you about it?" she

said, her voice deceptively calm. She leaned forward, anger staining her cheeks, her eyes flashing blue fire. "Two years, one month, and twenty-three days. But who's counting?"

"Brianna—" He began frowning.

"Two years ago, I was dating a wonderful man. I was crazy about him. Absolutely head over heels in love. I'd never been in love before, but I knew it was the real thing. I love him. I loved him then, I love him now. Came here for Thanksgiving that year and then— nothing. He never called me again. When I called him, he didn't return my calls, or brushed me off."

Josh looked uncomfortable.

Ruthlessly she continued, not giving him a chance to say a word. "I never knew why. So we stopped seeing each other. I could've dated other men, but I didn't care to spend my time with anyone else. I didn't want to date. I didn't want to search for another man to fall in love with. It would never be the same. I love Jake Morgan. I loved him then, I love him now. I will love him until the day I die."

"Oh, God," Josh said, rubbing his hand over his face, meeting his sister's eyes again, as if compelled to do so.

"Right. I've been desperately unhappy for a long time, Josh. And you know what? I just found out something that leads me to suspect you had something to do with that unhappiness."

She wanted to throw something to relieve the escalating tension. She stared at her brother, willing him to refute her charge. Willing him to say he hadn't a clue what she was talking about.

He stared at his sister for a long moment. "I meant it for the best," he said at last.

"Whose best? Yours? Certainly not mine." Tears shimmered in her eyes. She'd so hoped she was wrong, that neither of her brothers had done anything so horrible.

"Josh, I have been desperately unhappy for two years! I tried to hide it so you and Jase wouldn't worry. There was nothing you could do, so I thought. Now I want to know exactly what happened. What did you do? And why?"

She took a deep breath, trying to calm the raging turmoil. *What had her brother done?*

"Brianna, the man's a cop. You know how dangerous that kind of life is?"

"You don't like him because he's a cop?"

"It's a dangerous career. I want someone better for you. Someone who would show up each night after work, not someone to worry about every day."

"Is being a cop more dangerous than being a cowboy? More dangerous than a rodeo rider? Give me a break. It's not any more dangerous than a lot of professions. What am I supposed to do? Wait for a man who has a perfectly safe job, huh, Josh? And then make sure he never leaves the house in case a car careens out of control and kills him?" she asked sarcastically.

Their parents had been killed in just such a manner.

"What did you do, Josh? Besides ruin my chance for happiness. I want to know what you did."

He shoved back his chair and paced over to the

window, leaning his hands on the sill and gazing out into the dark yard.

"Not that much. If he'd cared for you, he'd have told me to go to hell and gone on seeing you. I called him and he backed off."

"I want to know what you told him."

She was feeling sick. Her brother had warned Jake off. She still couldn't believe it.

"I told him to stay away from my baby sister. That's what."

Josh slammed his hand down on the sill and turned.

"Someone has to watch out for you. You're too easy to take advantage of. You have a lot of money behind you. This ranch does very well. I wanted to make sure he wasn't some fortune hunting opportunist looking for a free ride. Cops don't make a lot of money."

"I don't believe it."

She stood and limped over until she faced Josh. Angrily she poked his chest with her index finger, afraid she would lose all self-control.

"Just because Jeannie tried to take you for all you had doesn't mean everyone else in the world is cut from the same cloth. Just because your fiancée was a gold digger doesn't mean any man who was interested in me would be. Damn you, how dare you interfere with my life?"

"I dared because I was worried about you."

"I'm a grown woman, perfectly capable of choosing my own path in life. I don't need or want any interference from my brother. Just because you were born a couple of years before me doesn't give you any rights over me, now or in the future. It's none of your business whom I see, whom I date or whom I marry. You got that clear, cowboy?" She poked his chest again.

He captured her finger and moved it away. "I did it for you, to protect you."

She snatched her hand away. "I don't know why you ever thought you had the right to interfere in my life, but you were *not* doing it for me. I don't need your protection! Was it a power trip or just jealousy that your sister found someone special and you were alone? Or were you just lashing out wherever you could because of Jeannie?"

He stared at her. "Leave Jeannie out of it. She had nothing to do with it. I thought you and Tom Bolton might make a go of it," he retorted. "He's got his own spread now. You and he were always close. At least I know he's not some fortune hunter."

"Tom and I were friends when we were in *high school.* I haven't seen him in years. In case it escapes your attention, my life is now in Texarkana at the college. Maybe one day in Austin at the university there, but I would no more want to marry a rancher than I would want to be one."

The enormity of what her brother had done was almost too much to grasp.

"Did you tell Jake I was seeing someone else?"

Josh gritted his teeth, his jaw muscles jumped. "I told him you were practically engaged to a man you'd known all your life. I told him you might be having a fling with him, but when the time came to marry, he wasn't even in the running."

She took a deep breath, the hurt almost too deep to bear. She'd expected support from her brothers, not betrayal. "You stay out of my life from now on, is that clear? I don't want to see you again. I don't want to talk to you for a long time. *Stay out of my life!*"

She snatched her hand away and stomped over to the coat rack. Yanking her jacket down, she donned it and turned.

"I'm sorry. I didn't know your feelings went so deep," he said, his expression contrite and sincere.

"Sorry isn't good enough, Josh. You never asked, did you? You just took charge and tried to run my life. I have spent the past two years alone. Maybe I'll spend the rest of my life alone because of your blasted interference. Stay away from me from now on!"

She ran in to the kitchen.

"We're leaving," she told Susan.

"Right now?" Her friend was startled. Though she had to hear the yelling voices.

"Exactly right now!" Brianna said.

Josh came into the kitchen. "No, don't go. Not like this. Talk to me Brianna. Let me see what I can do to make it right."

"You stay out of my life!'

"I'll get my coat." Susan said quietly.

Susan drove toward Texarkana, glancing once or twice at her friend. "Want to talk about it?"

"Not yet, I'm so angry I could spit nails!" Brianna replied. "Sorry to put you through this. You're a good friend."

"Yep, so remember that when you need someone to vent to."

Brianna nodded. Then despite her earlier words, she began to tell Susan all she'd discovered.

Ending with, "I can't believe my own brother would do such a thing to me."

Susan glanced at her again. "You're kidding, right? Your brothers have tried to run your life since your folks died. Just because you're all grown up doesn't mean they recognize that. Be glad it wasn't worse."

"I don't' see how it could be worse."

"Me either, but I bet it could be"

Brianna laughed at that. It didn't diminish her anger, but it did give her a second's respite from the churning adrenaline.

She wasn't sure how she was going to handle Jake, but she would set him straight on a few things the next time she saw him.

She also knew it would be a long time before she got over her anger or the sense of betrayal she felt from her brother. Far from having her back, he'd caused a major rift in her life.

Or had he? Had Jake used that excuse as a means of getting out of a relationship that was turning more serious than he wanted?

She loved him. He'd never said the words to her.

When she reached home, some of the tension had abated. She thanked Susan for being there for her, but told her she would be fine on her own that night.

Entering the house, Brianna saw there was a

message on her answering machine. Listening she heard Jake's voice asking her to call him.

She didn't want to call him. She wanted to see him. Tomorrow.

In the meantime, she had a lot to think about.

One thing Josh had said echoed over and over in her mind. If Jake had really cared about her, he'd have told her brother to go to hell and continued seeing her. But he hadn't.

She didn't like the thought, but maybe Josh was right. Maybe Jake really didn't care for her the way she wanted him to. Maybe he didn't love her the way she loved him.

Jake called just as she was dropping off to sleep.

"Where were you today?" he asked abruptly.

"I had errands to run," she replied vaguely. She was not going to tell him about Josh over the phone. She wanted to talk to him face-to-face. Maybe then she'd find out how he really felt.

"Driving all right?"

"Susan drove." She clutched the phone tightly, wishing she knew what to do, what to say.

Would Jake have stopped seeing her just on Josh's say-so?

"What's your schedule tomorrow?"

"My first class isn't until ten, but I'm going into the office around nine."

She wanted to see him but now wanted to stall. Once she confronted him with what Josh had done—then what?

If her brother's comment was right on, it'd make no

difference to Jake.

"We think we have a lead. You have someone there tonight? It'll probably all be over tomorrow."

"Who?"

"Tomorrow." With that, he hung up.

Blast the man, how did he expect her to sleep tonight worrying about whom they suspected? One of her students? Most likely, since it followed so soon after discovering the grades had been changed in her calculus class. But who?

Brianna dressed with care the next morning, trying to cover the dark circles beneath her eyes. She usually wore woolen slacks to work since it was so cold in winter. But today she chose a dusty pink woolen sweater paired with a dark brown skirt. She brushed her hair until it gleamed with highlights, applying enough makeup to hide the evidence of her sleeplessness. Dressing up had nothing to do with seeing Jake today.

The morning dragged by. He did not come, or call, before her first class. She watched the back of the classroom during the hour, thinking he might drop in as he had before.

He did not.

Working through lunch so she wouldn't miss him, she was beginning to worry when he finally showed up at her door.

"Hi." She looked up. Her heart raced and her hand grew damp. She'd practiced what she would say when she saw him, but suddenly her mind went blank. All she could do was stare at him and feel the electricity sparking through her. Would she ever get tired of looking at him?

Ever stop wanting him?

"Hi. Can I close the door?" he asked, cocking an eyebrow.

At her nod, he shut the door behind him and walked over to the chair across the desk from her.

"You found him," she said, noticing the seriousness of his expression.

"We found him. Alan Dalton. Know him?"

Slowly she shook her head. "The name doesn't ring a bell."

"Not surprising. He wasn't one of your students, though he does attend the university. He's Peggy Albert's boyfriend."

Instant understanding. "He changed her grade so she could keep her scholarship."

"Bingo. Apparently, without the scholarship she was out of school. Alan didn't want that for her or himself."

Brianna frowned. "So he risked jail to keep her in school?"

Jake nodded. "That's it. We've got a complete confession—breaking and entering, vandalism, malicious mischief, assault and battery, tampering with the computer, theft."

He shook his head. "He's twenty-one studying computer science. That's how he knew how to hack the college computer and alter the grades. He switched more than one to confuse the issue if anyone suspected anything. Then he had to get your grade sheets to make verification that much more difficult."

She sighed. "All for his girlfriend." Idly she rubbed her sore wrist. "What a sad ending for a young student with potential. And for a girlfriend who wouldn't have been in that situation if she had just done the work. What a waste."

"He said he was sorry for knocking you down. That was an accident. He only wanted to grab the briefcase and run."

She nodded. If she hadn't lost her balance, she wouldn't have fallen. He hadn't deliberately pushed her.

"Now what?" she asked.

"We're turning the case over to the D.A. His office will contact you. If there's a trial, it'll be in a couple of months. My guess is the kid will continue to admit he did it and there'll be a hearing and sentencing. But you don't have to worry anymore. The reasons for the break-ins are gone. He wanted your grade book, and when he couldn't find it in your house, he tried here, your car. Finally taking the briefcase."

"Thank you. You said you'd find the guy, and you did."

He stood. "Just part of the job."

"Wait. I wanted to talk to you."

Was he leaving? Just like that? The case was solved, so he was going?

Not if she had anything to say about it.

"About?" He remained standing, looking as if he'd bolt at any moment.

"About my brother, Josh. I went to see him yesterday."

Jake's expression didn't waver. He regarded her steadily as he stood before her desk. "And?"

"And he told me you two talked a couple of years

ago." She pushed back her chair and stood. It helped shorten the distance she had to look up at him. If he wouldn't sit, she'd stand.

Jake clenched his fists but remained silent.

The betraying gesture touched Brianna. Taking heart, she walked around her desk, her ankle scarcely aching. She'd hoped for a better reaction than this. But she had always hoped around Jake. It didn't often do any good.

"I never knew why you stopped calling me. I thought we were having fun. I enjoyed spending time with you." She stopped close enough to him that she could feel his heat, breathe his after-shave.

"Your brother set me straight on a few things, that's all. He's right. You and I don't have much in common." His voice was carefully neutral.

"Are you nuts? We get along fine. More than fine most times." She reached out and touched his cheek lightly. His hand snapped up and grabbed her wrist, pulling her away from him, his fingers lingering on her soft skin.

"What we had worked for a while. But Josh was right. We're too different to make a go of it. I'm a cop, Brianna. That's all I ever wanted to be. I make a good salary, but nothing to compare with the money you have from the Rafter C. And I'm old-fashioned enough to want to provide for my own family, not live off a rich wife. Besides, what happened to the man you were going to marry?"

The clenching of his teeth gave her a clue he was not as disinterested as his tone suggested.

She took heart. "That's plain dumb. First of all, I'm not rich. Weren't you listening when I told you I could finally afford a town house because of my second job at the Air Force base? I don't have lots of money from the Rafter C. I'm part owner with Josh and Jase, but most of the money's plowed back into the ranch. That's what keeps it going, keeps it up-to-date and modern. Secondly, there's no other man. There never was. Josh made that up."

"My job's too dangerous," he continued as if she hadn't spoken. "I know from wives of other cops that they worry constantly about their husbands. Living with that kind of fear is draining."

She tugged at her hand, but he didn't release her, his grip tightening instead. "You're as bad as Josh. No wonder you stayed away. You agree with him. I get it— life's dangerous. No one gets out alive. I could have been killed if I had hit my head hard enough the other morning. But I wasn't. You could be killed in a car crash like my parents, or fall off a ladder like your uncle. Nowhere does it say that anything in life is guaranteed. Except I can guarantee you that I love you."

His lips moved in a semblance of a smile, but it didn't reach his eyes. "Hero syndrome. I saved you, so you're grateful."

"Grateful be damned! Let me tell you something, Jake Morgan." The index finger of her other hand poked his chest, just as she had done with her brother. These men made her so angry she could scream.

"For the past two years, I haven't had a single date. Do you want to know why?" Without waiting for him to reply, she continued, "Because I didn't want to go out with anyone but you. I loved you then and I love you now. I've loved you all along. You may not love me and if that's the way of things, so be it. But if you feel anything for me, tell me. Jake, I love you."

He took her other hand and bent both behind her, pressing her body against his as he lowered his mouth to hers. His kiss was sweet. Gentle. Brief. Lifting up his head, he gazed down into her eyes for an endless moment as if imprinting her features in his mind for all time.

"You get on with your life, Brie. You've got a great future here at the college. You'll find a nice intellectual type to talk to and share your ideas with. I'm not for you, sweetheart, much as I wish I were. I don't know anything about family life. It was just my uncle and me for so long, then me alone. I'm a bad risk, any way you look at it. Listen to your brother, and me. Find someone else."

He kissed her again, then released her and turned.

She stood stock-still, staring in disbelief as he opened the door and walked down the long hallway. She moved slowly to the doorway and watched as he pressed the button for the elevator, then was swallowed up inside as the doors closed behind him.

He'd gone. He hadn't said he loved her. He had not replied to her confession of love at all. Not swept her off her feet and insisted he'd loved her all along.

Instead, he agreed with Josh.

Her heart felt as if it were breaking. She raised her palm to her chest and pressed hard, trying to assuage the ache. For the last few hours, she'd counted on Jake loving her.

She thought back over the past few weeks. He'd been so attentive. His kisses had melted all her resistance, and he had seemed to be struggling for control, as well. Had she totally misread the situation?

The elevator chimed. For one brief, heart-stopping moment, she thought he was coming back. Her heart soared. But two students stepped out and headed away from her. Sighing, she turned, closed the door behind her and let the tears fall.

Somehow, Brianna made it through the rest of the day. And for minutes at a time, she was able to forget Jake and the hopes she'd had of his admitting he loved her.

Even walking to her car, she couldn't help glancing around, hoping to see him waiting for her. Looking over the area reminded her of how he always scanned the vicinity whenever they went anywhere. How long this time would it take to get her life under some sort of control? To regain the sense of contentment she'd begun to forge?

There were two messages from Josh on her phone, which she'd turned off earlier, both demanding that she call him as soon as she got home. So not going to happen.

Her head ached a bit. She'd fix a light dinner, then lie down. She sighed. She remembered last time she'd been so depressed that sleep had been her only panacea. Was she going to repeat that remedy?

Just after nine, her phone rang. Brianna was lying on her bed, staring up at the ceiling. The hall light offered the only illumination. Slowly she reached out to answer the phone.

"Brianna?"

"Hi, Jase," she responded listlessly.

"What's up, baby sister?" he asked gently.

It was almost her undoing. Tears welled, but she fought to keep them from falling. Sitting up, she pushed her hand through her hair. "Life isn't much fun right now, big brother."

"So I hear from Josh. You okay?"

"Do you mean physically or emotionally?"

"Both."

"My ankle still hurts a little. My wrist is almost well. My head aches tonight, but I'm not sure that's from the bump or the fact I told Jake I loved him today and he told me he wasn't right for me." She brushed the tears that spiked her lashes and took a deep, shaky breath.

"Is he right?" Jase asked softly.

"No. But Josh put the notion into his head and Jake's stubborn. I have to admit he can be as cantankerous as that old mule Daddy used to have. But I don't mind."

She loved him happy, cranky, mad, stubborn. She wouldn't change anything except his answer that afternoon.

"And now you're mad at Josh."

"You cannot even imagine how angry I am at him. He had no right to interfere with my life. I can manage things fine. If I mess up, I have only myself to blame. Except in this, I blame Josh. I may never speak to him again. How could he do that to me?" Anger began to rise.

"He was just looking after his baby sister," Jase explained.

"Ha. I'm only two years younger than he is. I don't need looking after. Oh, Jase, I'm so lonely. I only want to spend time with Jake. These past two years have been hell. I keep as busy as I can with work and buying and fixing up this place, but it's not enough. Why can't he love me back?"

"Maybe it's for the best—Wait a minute."

"Brianna?" Her sister-in-law's voice came across the line.

"Hi, Shannon."

"Go away, Jase. This is girl talk." There were several seconds of silence, then Shannon spoke again. "Brianna, it seems to me these men have fouled things up royally."

Brianna smiled. Trust her petite sister-in-law to get right to the heart of the matter. Her brother stood well over six feet, yet his small, dark-haired wife had him wrapped around her little finger.

"You could say that. I can't forgive Josh for interfering. Nor Jake for agreeing with him."

"You know your own mind, no matter what they say. I think you'll forgive Josh sooner or later. He's your brother and his reason for interfering was sound, even if misguided. The question I have for you is what are you doing about the situation now?"

"What can I do? I told Jake I loved him and he walked away."

"So you're just giving up?"

"I don't know," Brianna said.

"I'm going to tell you a secret that you are never, never to let Jase know you know."

"Okay."

"When we were first married, your stubborn brother would not sleep with me. He was convinced I went along with the marriage solely out of gratitude. Stupid man, I was crazy about him from the first moment I saw him, even if he was a rodeo cowboy. Anyway, that's why I was so delighted when you and Josh came to spend that first Thanksgiving with us. With the two of you in the guest rooms, that left Jase no place else to go but to my room!"

Brianna smiled. She could just picture Shannon maneuvering her obstinate brother.

"So I get Jake over here somehow and force him into my bed?" she asked, trying to follow Shannon's train of thought.

Shannon giggled softly. "Maybe nothing that drastic. But you're a smart person. These men have no business making decisions for you. You make your own."

"Shannon, I owe you one. I've got an idea."

"You owe me nothing. Just find your happiness like I found mine with your brother."

Brianna hung up the phone a few minutes later, cheered beyond belief. Shannon was right. There was no reason for her to let Josh and Jake decide her fate. She was in charge of her life and she'd live it as she wanted.

And, if possible, with whom she wanted.

Returning to bed, she considered and discarded a dozen ideas. Finally, one came to mind that wouldn't be dislodged. She studied it from all angles. It'd work. She'd make sure it worked. And if Jake didn't like it, well, too bad. Time he learned what it was like to have someone else make the decisions.

The next morning, Brianna called the police station and asked to speak to Don Winston. After acknowledging she knew about the arrest and conferring about her testimony, she casually brought up Jake's name.

"He was such a help. Did he take the rest of his vacation time? I felt badly infringing on his free time," she said with false sincerity. She'd infringe on his time from now on, whenever she had the chance.

"Far as I know, he's still working. He returned to work yesterday. And he should have taken some time off. He's as grouchy as a bear."

"The weekend's coming up. He'll get some down time then. He's not working an extra shift or anything, is he?" she probed.

"Far as I know, he'll be off from Friday night until Monday."

"I'm so pleased you found the man responsible," she concluded. She hoped Don thought that was the only reason she called.

She smiled when she hung up. Jake was in town and had the weekend free. Friday would be the day.

Brianna made her plans carefully. Thursday she drove by his apartment to study the neighborhood. She stopped at four o'clock and parked in front of his building, watching the mothers walking their babies and the college students strolling home after classes. By four-twenty, the sidewalk was deserted.

Friday she shopped for groceries. Since Jake liked to

eat and she liked to cook, she bought plenty of supplies. She wanted everything to be special. If they ran out, they could shop together.

She packed carefully, making sure she took the most obviously feminine apparel she owned. She added only a couple of jeans and T-shirts. She was out to make a statement, not blend in.

The hard part lay ahead. Actually, there were two critical times—the break-in and the confrontation. But she was determined to come out on top both times. No more acquiescing to others. Shannon was right. It was time she took charge of her own life.

She drove to Jake's apartment building and parked on a side street. Casually strolling along the sidewalk, she was relieved to notice how deserted the neighborhood was. It boded well for her plan.

Skirting the side of the building, she stopped beneath Jake's bathroom window, the one he always kept open. About four inches of clearance showed. She glanced around, her heart tripping in double time. Nervous in case of discovery, she was not truly afraid. If she was caught, she doubted he'd press charges. At least she hoped he wouldn't.

Dragging over a trash can, she carefully balanced on its top and stood, holding on to the side of the brick building. Reaching for the window, she pushed it all the way up. Taking a deep breath, she placed her hands on the sill and jumped. Her left wrist screamed in agony. Before she collapsed, she thrust herself through the window. Resting on her stomach, her legs dangling, she withdrew her hand and shook it to ease the pain. She had obviously overestimated the healing.

In only another minute, she stood in his tub. Peeking out the window, she verified the area was still deserted. She scanned the windows of the adjacent houses that overlooked this side of the apartment building. She saw no one. Lowering the window, she beamed with success. Stage one accomplished.

Within ten minutes, she had unloaded her car. Another half hour had her clothes distributed in his closet and dresser. She put away the groceries and started dinner.

When she heard the front door open, she held her breath. Slowly she turned from the stove and faced the living room. This was it.

Jake walked in, paused, then looked at her, his dark eyes blazing, his body alert and poised as if for attack.

"What the hell are you doing here?" he demanded.

Eleven

"Right here, right now?" she asked, stalling. "I'm cooking dinner." She took a deep breath and boldly walked over to him, holding eye contact the entire time. She could see the emotions dance across his face before he schooled his features. Daringly, she reached up and pulled his head down for a kiss.

His lips were cool, his cheeks cold. She opened her mouth and he responded instantly, his own moving possessively over hers as his arms drew her tightly against him.

Jake kissed her long and deep, breaking away only when breathing became difficult for both of them.

"What are you doing here?" He rested his forehead against hers, rubbing his nose against hers. His tone was soft, his eyes delving deep into hers.

"Cooking dinner?" she returned, hesitant to take the final step.

"And just how did you get in?"

She smiled saucily, her eyes dancing in delight. "There are always ways. Why doesn't the famous detective figure it out for himself?"

He thought a moment. "The bathroom window?"

She nodded. "For that you win the prize. Me." Reaching up, she brushed her lips across his again, then pulled back. "And dinner. I'm cooking beef Stroganoff. I made a deep-dish cherry pie for dessert." It was his favorite, that she remembered.

"Why are you here, Brianna?" he asked as he shrugged off his jacket and tossed it across the sofa.

She turned back to the kitchen, keeping busy lest her courage fail. "For one thing, I wanted to see you again. For another, I thought a nice dinner would be a kind of thank-you for watching out for me while Alan was running amok."

"I don't need thanks."

"Right, you were only doing your job. I heard you say that the other morning. Maybe I want to cook dinner for you." Maybe do a lot of things for you.

"All right, then you go home."

"Actually, home is where your heart is. I have a house a few blocks over. But my home is here with you." She turned and faced him defiantly. "And here is where I'm staying."

He shook his head. "You can't stay here."

"Wanna bet? I've already moved in." She tilted her chin arrogantly. Curious to see what he would do next.

"What?" His voice was low, incredulous.

"Check it out," she said flippantly, gesturing toward his bedroom.

In two seconds he was in the room. In ten he was back.

"You can just pack up your things and get out. Have you gone nuts?"

She smiled slowly, hoping he couldn't see the rapid beat of her heart. She dared not let him know how nervous she felt or she wouldn't stand a chance.

"Actually, I've decided I'm a bit tired of others running my life for me, so I thought I'd take over for a while. I'm twenty-six, you know, Jake. Don't you think it's time I was in charge of me?"

"I know how old you are. What does that have to do with anything?" He crossed the room and crowded her into the kitchen.

She held her ground, refusing to back up or give way.

"It has to do with not needing anyone to tell me how to live or what's good for me. I don't need my brother choosing my boyfriends. I don't need the man I love acting like an altruistic fool and telling me what's good for me. I'm the only one who knows what's good for me. And I'm taking a stand tonight. Here I stay!"

He was silent, weighing her declaration, searching for something as he gazed deep into her eyes. He noted her determined stance, her stubborn chin and the fierce emotion reflected in her deep blue eyes.

Slowly he nodded, reaching out to touch her skin, to feather his fingertips across her cheek, push her hair behind her ear, trace that strong jaw.

"Nothing's changed. I don't have a lot of money."

"I'm not independently wealthy. I told you, the ranch takes back most of the money it earns."

"I don't know much about family life. It was just my uncle and me, and he wasn't much on family stuff."

"I know lots, more than I want to sometimes,

especially about nosy brothers who don't mind their own business. We'll make our own family, establish our own traditions and customs. You'll like Jase and Shannon. And right now, Josh isn't a problem. I may never speak to him again."

"My job is still hazardous."

"So, apparently, is mine. When was the last time you were in the hospital? And didn't you tell me your uncle died off duty? I expect most cops retire and only a few die in the line of duty. We'll take our chances."

"Will we be able to blend our life-styles? I liked meeting your friends at the reception. Did you like my friends when we went out to dinner?"

Her gaze dropped to his chin. "Except for Diane," she mumbled.

He raised her head with his finger beneath her chin. "I told you there was nothing between us."

"I didn't come here to discuss your old girlfriends." She tossed her hair, waiting. *Waiting.*

"So you thought a *fait accompli* would accomplish what you wanted. Move in and leave me no choice?"

"You didn't give me any choice. You decided something was good for me and walked away. I think this is good for both of us and I'm not walking away." Could she pull it off?

"Your brother's right. You could do better than me."

"I don't think so."

Slowly he smiled, giving in. "All right. But on one condition."

She blinked, her heart threatening to burst. *All right?* He said it was *all right?* Happiness swept through her. She longed to throw herself into his arms, but caution held her back.

"What condition?" she asked warily.

"That we get married before you move in," he said simply.

From walking away from her to marriage in one conversation was almost too much to take in!

She stared, unable to breathe, unable to think.

Jake's smile broadened. His thumb brushed her lower lip, tugging gently.

"Say yes," he urged, a moment of uncertainty setting in. Surely this was what she wanted. He knew beyond all doubt it was what he wanted.

"Yes," she repeated. "Are you sure?"

"Of what? That I want you to marry me? Yes, I'm sure. I was going to ask you two years ago, at Christmas. I thought that would be romantic. And I wanted to give you some romance.

Then your brother stopped by after you'd left for Thanksgiving, and told me you were practically engaged to another man. The man was a rancher and you'd be happier with someone you'd known all your life. Josh suspected my motives were mercenary, that my job was too uncertain to offer stability to a woman like you. He said your family wouldn't stand by if I continued seeing you. I guess I let pride and anger stand in the way of common sense. You're right. You're totally grown. If you know what you want, who am I to say otherwise?"

"I sure hope there's something more," she murmured, stepping into his embrace, reveling in the feel of his strong body, the sensation of homecoming that was so strong.

"Like I love you, Brie? Like I've loved you for years, missed you so much I couldn't sleep nights."

"Something like that," she nodded, resting her cheek against his. "Don't stop."

He chuckled as his hands traced the firm muscles of her back, rubbing up and down, pressing her firmly against him.

"How about I used to cruise down Sheridan Avenue when you lived in the apartment over there, just to see you start for school? How about I haven't been to Magio's since the day we had dinner there? And it was once my favorite restaurant. How about I'm only human and can stand only so much? There comes a time when a man knows when it's best to grab the future with both hands and hold on, whatever the risk."

"Umm, better and better." Happiness flooded her. Tears pricked. She burrowed closer, clinging. *Love you, love you, love you* her heart pumped rhythmically.

"How about I love you more than I thought it possible to love anyone? I want you more than anything." His low, sexy voice was intoxicating.

"I love you, too, Jake. I hate the time we've spent apart."

The time for talking was over.

He kissed her.

The timer sounded for endless minutes before either recognized the sound.

"Dinner," she said, pulling away and turning to the stove.

"After dinner, we'll move your things back to your

house."

She turned, stricken. "No, we won't. I told you I was staying, and I meant it."

"I said we'd marry first, and I meant it. I don't want your two brothers showing up and finding all your things at my place."

"Scared?"

"Yep."

She laughed at his teasing, wondering if Jake was ever afraid of anything. Except maybe committing his heart.

"I love you," she said clearly. She wanted to make sure he knew that for all time.

"I know you do. I love you. After dinner, I'll show you how much."

In the end, Jake had his way. They moved her things back to her home later that evening.

"How attached are you to your apartment?" Brianna asked as they hung the last of her dresses.

"I've lived there for ten years, but it's only an apartment. Why?"

"Want to move in here?" she asked.

He looked around, then at her. "I could."

"Well, you're bringing the cabin to the marriage. I thought I could offer this."

"Are we bargaining?"

"Not really. I just don't want to live in an apartment again. I like my house. But if your pride demands that we live in your poky old apartment—"

He laughed, snatched her up and spun her around and around until she was dizzy. "I like this place. And no, my pride doesn't demand that we stay in my poky old apartment. It doesn't matter where we live at first, because before too long we are going to want a bigger place."

"We are?"

"For the kids."

Her heart melted. "Kids?"

"At least a half dozen," he said firmly.

"Wow, we'd better get started." Laughing happily, she tightened her arms around his neck and kissed him.

Epilogue

Shannon Hart readjusted the skirt, settling the folds to her satisfaction. Standing back, she smiled at Brianna. "You look beautiful. Of course, I've never seen you when you didn't, but today especially so."

"Just as long as Jake thinks so," Brianna said, staring at herself in the full-length mirror. The long white dress was a dream. The lacy sleeves covered her arms to her wrists; the fitted bodice enhanced her slender figure. She could hear the organ playing softly, the murmur of the guests. In less than ten minutes she would walk down the aisle and marry Jake Morgan.

She could hardly believe this was happening. It had been endless weeks since January. While she agreed six weeks wasn't too long to plan a wedding—scarcely long enough as it proved—she would have been satisfied with a quick marriage the week after he proposed.

Jake had insisted on a big wedding. They had invited almost the entire college staff and every law enforcement officer in the county. There were longtime family friends to be included from home, cowboys from the ranch, and the church was threatened with a standing-room-only crowd.

"Jase's right outside. You ready?" Shannon asked. She smoothed her own deep rose gown over her hips. She was Brianna's sole attendant.

"As I'll ever be." Brianna took a deep breath and reached for her bouquet. There was no reason to be nervous. She loved Jake, he loved her, and today they would join their lives together.

Shannon opened the door and slipped out. Before it could close, Jase and Josh walked in together. In the dark suits and white shirts neither man looked like the rough and tumble cowboys she was used to. They both looked amazing and she was filled with happiness, though her expression grew wary when her gaze rested on Josh.

"What are you doing here?" she asked.

"I've come to walk up the aisle with my brother to give my sister to the man she loves," Josh said. "We're her only family right now and we want to give her away together."

Tension shimmered in the air as he waited for Brianna's response. The tightening of his jaw gave away the uncertainty he felt.

Brianna blinked back tears, pressing her lips together tightly so she wouldn't cry.

"I love you, Sis. I'm glad things worked out for you," Josh added softly. "Despite the mess I made of things."

She reached out to hug him. Then turned to Jase and hugged him, tears sparkling on her lashes.

"None of that." Jase brushed the tears away. "We don't want everyone to think we're forcing you to marry the man."

"Or that you're having regrets," Josh said, smiling

warmly at his younger sister.

"I'm so happy today. Be happy with me," she whispered, love for both her brothers almost matching the love she had for Jake.

"We are," Josh answered. "We are. Now the question is, can Jake ride?"

"Who cares? We're not living on a ranch. We're living right here in Texarkana"

"Weekends?" Jase asked.

"At our cabin in the mountains."

"Summers?" Josh asked.

"Well, we'll visit once in a while, but our future is here. And mine is with him."

Of that there was no doubt. She loved Jake, always had, always would.

The organ music changed.

"Time to go, Brianna."

Linking her arms with those of her two tall brothers, she smiled radiantly and started down the aisle to meet Jake.

As he waited, his dark eyes caught hers and held as she walked steadily toward him and their future together.

—The End—

I hope you enjoyed *Tangled Hearts.* If so, would you be so kind as to leave a review at the vendor where you purchased it? Reviews can be long or short, they are always a help. Thank you.

Books in THE HARTS OF TEXAS Series

Rebel Heart (Book 1)

Tangled Hearts (Book 2)

Reckless Heart (Book 3)

Please visit my website: www.barbaramcmahon.com
for a complete list of all my books.